HOW I SURVIVED MIDDLE SCHOOL

Who's Got Spirit?

Check out these other books in the
How I Survived Middle School series by Nancy Krulik

Can You Get an F in Lunch?

Madame President

I Heard a Rumor

The New Girl

Cheat Sheet

P.S. I Really Like You

HOW I SURVIVED MIDDLE SCHOOL

Who's Got Spirit?

By Nancy Krulik

SCHOLASTIC INC.

New York   Toronto   London   Auckland   Sydney
Mexico City   New Delhi   Hong Kong   Buenos Aires

For Ian and Amanda, who are incredibly spirited all the time!

No part of this publication may be reproduced, stored in a retrieval system, or transmitted in any form or by any means, electronic, mechanical, photocopying, recording, or otherwise, without written permission of the publisher. For information regarding permission, write to Scholastic Inc., Attention: Permissions Department, 557 Broadway, New York, NY 10012.

ISBN-13: 978-0-545-05257-3
ISBN-10: 0-545-05257-2

Published by Scholastic Inc. SCHOLASTIC and associated logos are trademarks and/or registered trademarks of Scholastic Inc.

12 11 10 9 8 7 6   9 10 11 12 13/0

Printed in the U.S.A.
First printing, September 2008
Book design by Alison Klapthor

Who's Got Spirit? Come On, Let's Hear It!

Let's face it, some kids have school spirit, and some just don't want to hear about it. Where do you fall on the school spirit scale? Take this quiz and find out.

1. **You just found out your school is having a pep rally during last period to cheer the football team to victory. What's _your_ game plan?**

   A. Rush into the bathroom and use your eye shadow and lipstick to paint your face in the school colors.
   B. Hurry to the nurse and pretend to be sick. You may as well get sent home early. You won't be missing anything, anyway.
   C. Text your BFF and ask her to save you a seat in the center of the bleachers because you're running a little late.

2. **It's the tradition to sing your school song at every home game. When the band starts playing, what do you do?**

   A. Rush off to the hot dog stand. The line's usually shortest during the song.
   B. Sing out, loud and proud.
   C. Sort of mumble syllables that kind of sound like the words of the song. Hey, at least you know the tune.

3. **You have a group English project that requires poster board, colored pencils, and different types of fabric. On Saturday, you and your friends head to the mall for a crafty shopping spree. How do you show off your school pride?**

   A. You wear your school jackets so everyone knows where you hail from.
   B. You tell people you go to a different school — yours is soooo lame.
   C. You don't. You just buy everything you need for the project, and then refuse to give school another thought. After all, it's Saturday!

4. **Your school is having a bake sale to raise cash for new uniforms for the field hockey and soccer teams. How do you pitch in?**

   A. You buy plenty of cupcakes and cookies. You're all for supporting the cause — and your sweet tooth!
   B. You pass the table by. You'd rather spend your cash on pizza!

C. You stay up all night baking cookies and cupcakes and decorating them with the school colors. The prettier they are, the more people will buy.

5. The principal just announced that the huge homecoming dance is next Friday night. What's the first thing you do?

A. Make other plans. Why be at school on a Friday night? You were there all week!

B. Sign up for the decorating committee.

C. Shop for a new dress, of course.

6. It's the afternoon of your school's championship basketball game. Where are you?

A. In the stands, cheering your team to V-I-C-T-O-R-Y!

B. In the hall outside the gym, selling pennants, T-shirts, and pom-poms. You've got to raise cash for *all* of your school teams.

C. On the court at the local playground, playing your own game of hoops.

7. Major bummer! Someone from a rival school has spray-painted mean graffiti on the outside wall of your school. How do you react to seeing it?

A. You don't really care — it's not what's outside the school that matters, it's what's going on inside.

B. You keep your eyes and ears open, searching for clues as to who the culprit might be.

C. You organize a clean-up committee and start scrubbing. You want to make sure everyone who passes the school is impressed with what an incredibly nice place it is.

8. It's student council election day. What are you doing?

A. Anxiously awaiting the results. You're running for treasurer!
B. Voting, of course.
C. Eating a sandwich in the cafeteria. School elections are a total waste of time.

So where do you fall on the school spirit meter? Add up your score and find out.

1.	A) 3	B) 1	C) 2
2.	A) 1	B) 3	C) 2
3.	A) 3	B) 1	C) 2
4.	A) 2	B) 1	C) 3
5.	A) 1	B) 3	C) 2
6.	A) 2	B) 3	C) 1
7.	A) 1	B) 2	C) 3
8.	A) 3	B) 2	C) 1

19-24 points: Who's got spirit? You! That's who! You are totally true to your school, and you want everyone to know it.

14-18 points: You definitely know your school rocks. You just don't always feel the need to scream and shout about it.

8-13 points: School spirit just isn't part of your curriculum.

Chapter
ONE

WELCOME TO SPIRIT WEEK!

THE RED-AND-WHITE BANNER was the first thing I saw when I got off the bus at Joyce Kilmer Middle School on Monday morning. It was hard to miss. The sign was humongous!

"I guess that's a *little* reminder, just in case you forgot." My friend Felicia giggled as she pointed to the massive sign.

How could I have forgotten? How could *anyone* have forgotten? Spirit Week was all everyone had been talking about since Principal Gold had announced it last Friday.

I'm a sixth grader at Joyce Kilmer Middle School. I've never been part of a Spirit Week before. So the minute I heard about it, I ran home and looked it up in the middle school handbook they'd given out at the sixth grade orientation. Unfortunately, the handbook didn't tell me much. It just said that Spirit Week was five days of fun, and a way for everyone to show how much school spirit they had.

The handbook also recommended that everyone wear red and white to school on Spirit Week days. Not very much information, huh? If there's one thing I've learned for sure since I've been in middle school, it's that the orientation handbook doesn't tell you a whole lot about what life in middle school is *really* like.

"Hey, yo! Jenny! Felicia! Happy Spirit Week!" my friend Chloe shouted as she came running over to Felicia and me.

I started laughing the minute I spotted her. Chloe was wearing yet another one of her hilarious T-shirts. This one was white with red letters. It said *Because I'm the Queen, That's Why!*

"That is so you," I told Chloe.

"I know," she agreed. "But I'm actually wearing it because it's red and white. It shows I've got school spirit."

"It shows you're bossy," Felicia joked.

Chloe didn't get mad. She knew Felicia was just teasing her. She also knew it was the truth. Chloe *was* kind of bossy. But we liked her that way. "Nice ribbons," she complimented me.

I reached up and touched the red and white ribbons that I'd braided into my hair. They were *my* way of showing school spirit. "Thanks. I got the idea from middleschoolsurvival.com," I told her. "I just searched for hairstyles, and there it was."

"Awesome!" Felicia said.

Middleschoolsurvival.com is my favorite website. It's filled with quizzes, recipes, crafts, and style ideas that are only for middle schoolers. I don't know how I would've gotten through the beginning of sixth grade without it.

Chloe looked over at Felicia. "Where's your red and white?" she asked her.

Felicia pulled up her pant legs. "Here," she said, showing off her red-and-white candy-cane striped socks. "They were the only clean clothes I had that were red and white. I haven't worn these socks since last Christmas."

"Maybe you should roll your jeans up to your knees so everyone can see them," Chloe suggested.

Felicia rolled her eyes. "Oh, right. That'd be stylish," she said sarcastically. "Can you just imagine what the Pops would say about that?"

Chloe shrugged. "Who cares?" she asked.

I knew Felicia cared. I would've cared. So would just about everyone else in our school. We all are concerned with what the Pops think. It's stupid, I know. But we care. The Pops rule our school.

Every school has their own group of Pops. They're the ones who wear the coolest clothes, have the best makeup, and only hang out with one another. They're at the top of the middle school social food chain. And everyone wants to be like them.

Now don't get me wrong. I have a lot of good friends. We eat lunch together, hang out on the weekends, and call one another's cell phones all the time. In fact, I probably have more friends than the Pops do. But no one would *ever* say I'm a Pop. At my school it's not the number of friends you have that makes you popular. You can't be really popular unless people want to get into your group. And no one at school was trying to get into my group of friends.

But nearly everyone wanted to be a Pop. People copied the way they dressed and the way they talked. They followed them around the school, and invited them to their birthday parties, hoping they would show up, even if just for a few minutes. Being able to say that the Pops were coming to your party was a social success guarantee.

But social success wasn't something Chloe was the least bit interested in. She was just happy being Chloe. That was what I loved most about her. The Pops meant nothing to her — unless they did something to really crack her up. Like now, for instance.

"Oh, man, check out the Pops," she said, laughing as she pointed toward the far end of the parking lot.

I looked over to where Chloe was pointing. The Pops were gathered in a big sea of red and white. In fact, they were all wearing exactly the same thing. Short white skirts and red T-shirts. My mouth dropped open wide when I saw what Addie Wilson was wearing. "Hey! That's *my* shirt!" I exclaimed.

It really shouldn't have come as a surprise that Addie Wilson — super Pop — was wearing something that belonged to me. She and I had always traded clothes with each other. Why not? We once were best friends. *Inseparable.*

Shocking, huh? But it's true. Jenny McAfee and Addie Wilson were BFF! Notice I used the word *were.* Addie and I haven't been best friends since we started middle school. While I was away at sleepaway camp last summer, Addie made a whole bunch of new friends. Now she was a Pop, and I wasn't. So our friendship was over.

Oh, and news flash: Addie was apparently also a T-shirt thief.

"You should go over there and make Addie give your shirt back right now!" Chloe suggested gleefully.

"And what's she supposed to wear all day?" I asked Chloe.

Chloe shrugged. "Who cares? She could always change into her smelly gym shirt."

"Oh, right," Felicia said. "Like Addie Wilson would ever wear *that* around the school."

"She doesn't even wear her gym shirt in gym *class,*" I told Choe and Felicia. "She always tells Coach that it's in the wash. I heard her whisper to Dana Harrison that she refuses to be seen in a gray shirt. It doesn't complement her skin tone or something."

Chloe rolled her eyes. "Give me a break."

"You gotta hand it to the Pops, though," Felicia pointed out. "They really organized themselves. No other group is going to have matching outfits. Look at the three of us. All we have are some ribbons, a shirt, and striped socks."

"Yeah, well, it's not like I can picture Marc and Josh wearing white skirts." I pointed out to her.

Felicia giggled. "Josh does have great legs, though," she joked. "It's all that tae kwon do!"

I thought about how embarrassed Josh would be if he had heard that. Everyone knew that he and Felicia were boyfriend and girlfriend. And Josh *knew* everyone knew. Still, he didn't like it very much when Felicia talked about it.

Just then, the first bell rang. There was no more time to talk about the Pops, striped socks, or boys in skirts. We had just five minutes to get to class. Spirit Week had officially begun!

By lunchtime, everyone had noticed the Pops' uniforms. They were hard to miss. I looked over at their table – the one near the windows where they sat every day. It looked as though a giant red-and-white cloud had fallen from the sky and landed in the middle of our school cafeteria. They'd even found a way for the guys they hung out with to get with the program. Instead of skirts, they were all wearing white shorts. Funny, that hadn't occurred to Felicia, Chloe, and me this morning.

On the other hand, my crowd of friends was . . . well . . . it wasn't that we didn't have spirit. It was just that we didn't have *organized* spirit. But what we lacked in uniforms we made up for in creativity. I had my red and white ribbons and Chloe had her T-shirt. But that was nothing compared to my friend Samantha. She'd actually dyed a red stripe on the left side of her hair and bleached a white one on the right.

"Wow!" I exclaimed as I sat down with my tray of red hot dogs, white rolls, white milk, and a red apple. Apparently, the cafeteria staff was into Spirit Week as well. "Check out your hair, Sam!"

"My mum thought I'd gone completely bonkers when I did it," Sam told me. "But I think it looks fab!"

Sam always talks like that. She just moved here from England. Her slang takes a little getting used to, but after a while it's pretty easy to translate. She'd just told me that her mom thought she was nuts for dyeing stripes into her hair, but she thought it looked awesome. And so did I.

"It's so cool," I assured her. "I wish my mom would let me dye my hair. But she won't even let me wear lip gloss to school. I doubt red and white dye is anywhere in my future."

"I think your ribbons are adorable," my friend Liza complimented me. "And they're sort of like hair dye that comes out."

I smiled. That was Liza, always finding a way to make everyone feel good about themselves. It was one of her greatest talents. Her other great talent was art. And judging from the sparkly red lion on her white tank top, I could tell she'd put that talent to use for Spirit Week.

"Did you make that?" I asked her.

Liza nodded. "It wasn't that hard. I just poured some red glitter on the fabric paint before it dried."

I sighed. *It wasn't that hard.* Like just anyone could paint a lion freehand the way she had. Sometimes I wanted to shake Liza and make her realize what an incredible artist she was.

"You know, we could earn a lot of money making T-shirts," Chloe suggested to Liza.

"We?" Liza asked her.

"Sure. You could do the art, and I could come up with the funny sayings," Chloe told her. "And with the right marketing plan . . ."

"What get-rich-quick scam is Chloe up to now?" Josh asked, as he took a seat next to Liza at our table.

I took one look at him and began to laugh. He was wearing a red T-shirt with a white math formula printed across the front: $a^2+b^2=c^2$. "What's that?" I asked him.

"The Pythagorean theorem," he answered, sounding surprised that I hadn't recognized it.

But I had never seen it before. And I knew there was no point asking Josh what that pytha-*whatever* was. Josh is a math whiz. He's already in seventh grade math even though he's a sixth grader like me. And he's getting an A+ in the class. His T-shirt was really funny, though. Not Chloe T-shirt funny, but different. *Josh* funny. And it was red and white, too.

"I'm talking about starting a T-shirt business with Liza," Chloe told him. "She'd be the talent and I'd be the brains."

"Gee, thanks a lot," Liza groaned. Liza's too nice to ever

be totally sarcastic, but I could tell that comment had annoyed her. Despite Chloe's claim that she'd be the brains of the operation, Liza's the *really* smart one. She just has a learning disability that sometimes makes school hard for her. But now she's got a tutor to help her, and it's definitely working. A few weeks ago our whole school took this major history test. Liza got the highest score in the seventh grade! That means she's going to represent our school in a statewide competition next month!

"You know what I mean," Chloe said. "We could make a fortune, Liza. All we have to do is come up with some cute shirts, and then advertise. We could do a website. Marc could videotape a commercial. . . ."

"Which *you'd* star in, right?" Sam asked her.

"Of course," Chloe said. "After all, I'm the one who was in the school play. And then . . ." She stopped for a minute and looked around. "Hey where is Marc, anyway?"

"I don't know," I said. "He's usually at lunch early, and so are the twins. But they're not here, either."

As if on cue, my friends Marilyn and Carolyn arrived at the table with their food trays in hand.

"You guys look so cute," I said, admiring the twins' spirit week outfits. Marilyn was wearing white jeans and a red, long-sleeve button-down shirt. Carolyn was wearing red jeans and a white, long-sleeve button-down.

"They're the same outfits we wore to the basketball championship," Marilyn told me.

"We just switched," Carolyn added. "Today I'm in the white shirt."

"And I'm in the red one," Marilyn said, finishing her sister's thought.

I nodded and pretended I'd noticed the switch. But the truth was, Marilyn and Carolyn looked pretty much the same. I would've had to work really hard to remember which twin was wearing which shirt at the game.

"Do you guys know where Marc is?" Chloe asked them, trying to turn the subject back to her new pet project. "I want to talk to him about this T-shirt thing.

"Chloe, I don't have time to start a business right now," Liza said gently. "I have a lot of schoolwork to concentrate on. . . ."

"Seriously," Carolyn agreed. "*Mega* work. And we have those projects for the . . ."

"Science fair," Marilyn added, finishing what Carolyn had begun to say.

"That's going to take up a lot of time," Liza agreed.

"Science fair?" I asked. "We have a science fair?" Funny, I must have missed that in the handbook, too.

The twins nodded. "We already had our partners assigned," Marilyn said.

"Marc's probably still in the science classroom with Mrs. Arlington," Carolyn suggested. "She had a long line of people waiting to receive a partner for their project."

"We don't get to choose our partners?" Chloe asked. She sounded very bummed.

"Oh, you do," Liza assured her. "It's just the seventh grade that gets assigned. Mrs. Arlington thinks it works better that way. I've got Chuck Parker for a partner."

"I've got Liana Morris," Carolyn said.

"And I have Janine Saperstein," Marilyn added.

"Boy, this is some day," I said. "First Spirit Week starts, and now the science fair. Pretty cool."

"Speaking of cool . . ." Liza joked.

I looked up. At just that moment the cloud of red-and-white Pops blew by our table on their way to the girls' room. No surprise there. The Pops always headed to the girls' room during lunch. But it wasn't for the reason you might think. They didn't actually use the bathroom. They just went there to put on makeup and gossip. It was sort of like their clubhouse.

But before the Pops made it to the door, they were stopped by Arielle Samson, a seventh grade non-Pop. "Those skirts are adorable," Arielle said sweetly.

"Of course they are," Sabrina said. "We wouldn't wear them if they weren't."

I rolled my eyes. Of all the Pops, Sabrina was the nastiest.

"What do *you* want?" Claire asked Arielle.

Okay, Claire could be sort of nasty, too.

"I was just wondering where you got your outfits," Arielle asked. She sounded intimidated.

"None of your business," Sabrina barked at her.

Addie sighed heavily. "Look, Arielle. We worked hard to put together our look. It was our idea to wear matching clothes. We don't want anyone else dressing this way. Why don't you and your crowd come up with something else to do?"

And with that, the Pops moved on, leaving Arielle just standing there. She seemed totally crushed, which I'm sure was exactly what the Pops had had in mind.

Carolyn's eyes were wide open. She looked furious. So did Marilyn.

"Oh, like they're the first people to wear matching clothes!" Marilyn blurted out.

"They are *so* not!" Carolyn agreed furiously.

"We do that a lot!" Marilyn insisted.

"Like at the championship game," Carolyn added.

"They stole it from us!" the twins exclaimed together.

I frowned. Just because the twins had worn matching clothes before anyone else, it didn't mean they were the ones who had started the trend. I silently added another rule to my never ending list of things they don't tell you in the middle school handbook.

MIDDLE SCHOOL RULE #26:

IT DOESN'T MATTER WHO STARTED SOMETHING. IT'S NOT A TREND UNTIL EVERYONE ELSE WANTS TO DO IT, TOO. AND THAT USUALLY STARTS WITH THE POPS.

Yep. Once again, Addie and her pals had gotten credit for something someone else had thought of. Or make that *taken* credit. And they were never going to admit it. There was only one thing my friends and I could do.

"We'll just have to come up with something better," I told them. "We'll do something really special for Spirit Week tomorrow."

"Tomorrow's hat day," Liza said. "Maybe we could all wear the same hats. We could get plain white baseball caps at the craft store and paint them."

"Everyone will be wearing hats," Chloe pointed out. "We have to stand out."

"Like the Pops," Liza agreed. "They look like cheerleaders."

"This is the one week a year I wish we had real cheerleaders." Marilyn sighed. "Then we wouldn't need those faux ones," Carolyn agreed.

I knew what she meant. Our middle school doesn't have cheerleaders, so the Pop pep squad that had just walked by was the closest thing we had at the moment.

"Cheerleaders!" Chloe exclaimed. "That's it! We'll make pom-poms and come up with a cheer."

Josh shook his head. "Count me out," he said. "Cheerleading's not my thing."

I laughed. Somehow I couldn't see him or our friend Marc waving pom-poms in the air. Sure, I know there are guy cheerleaders. But *my* guy friends would never be into that. "That's okay. We'll take care of the pom-poms," I assured him. "You can help make hats."

"Deal," Josh agreed. "And I'm sure Marc will film any cheer you guys do."

I was pretty sure of that, too. Marc wanted to be a director when he grew up. He was in the middle of making his first movie – a documentary about life in middle school. Kind of like MTV's *The Real World*, except with kids. Spirit Week would make a great addition to the film. I made a mental note to fill him in on our plans later.

"There's just one problem," Sam said. "We don't know how to make pom-poms."

Oops. I hadn't thought of that.

"That's no problem," Chloe said.

"It isn't?" I asked her.

"Of course not. We'll just look it up on middleschool survival.com," Chloe replied.

A few hours later, my girls and I were all gathered in my living room. We were surrounded by red glittery fabric paint, plain white baseball caps, and plenty of white plastic garbage bags. That's right, *garbage bags*! We were using them to make our pom-poms. That was what the website had told us to do.

As Liza painted our school logo on the baseball caps, the rest of us studied the directions I'd printed out for making pom-poms.

Rah! Rah!
Make Your Own Pom-Poms!

YOU WILL NEED:
- 20 small white trash bags
- scissors
- duct tape

HERE'S WHAT YOU'LL DO:
1. Lay 10 bags flat, one on top of another.
2. Line the bags up evenly.
3. Cut the pile of plastic garbage bags into small strips. Cut your strips only halfway up. The width of the strips can vary depending on how full you want the pom-pom to be. The thinner you cut the strips, the fuller the pom-pom will look.
4. Fold the pile of bags lengthwise. Wrap the duct tape very firmly around the uncut end of the pile. This is the handle. Below the tape handle are the pom-pom strips.
5. Now fluff up the pom-pom. Moisten your hands slightly, then take a few strips in the palms of your hands and rub them together for three minutes. The thicker you want the pom-pom, the longer you should rub the strips together.
6. To make the second pom-pom, take the remaining 10 bags and repeat steps 1 through 5.

"Pass the scissors," my friend Rachel said, after reading the printout. "Felicia and I can cut the bags."

"Cool," I said, passing a pair of scissors over to her. Rachel and Felicia have a different lunch period than I do, but I had made sure to let them know our plans.

"The Pops are going to freak when we walk in with these," Felicia said, as she cut a pile of bags into strips.

"And I'm working on a really great cheer," Chloe said. "Anyone know a word that rhymes with *Kilmer*?"

"How about saying Joyce Kilmer Middle School?" Sam suggested. "Then you can rhyme it with *cool* or *rule*."

Chloe frowned. "Well, sure, if you want to do it the *easy* way," she said. But I could tell she was definitely considering Sam's suggestion.

"Have you guys heard the one about the ghost who joined the cheerleading squad?" my pal Rachel asked us.

"Nope," Liza said.

"He wanted to add a little team spirit!" Rachel exclaimed. She burst out laughing at her own joke. The rest of us laughed, too. But not quite as much.

Felicia smiled and threw a roll of duct tape in Rachel's direction. "One more bad joke like that and we're going to use this to tape your mouth shut," she teased playfully.

Rachel laughed. "No problem," she replied. "I don't know that many cheerleading jokes, anyway." She began wrapping the duct tape around the uncut end of a pile of bags to make a handle, just like the website had instructed.

About an hour later, we had a big pile of white pom-poms on the floor. Two neat rows of painted baseball caps were drying on my back porch, and Chloe was pretty much done with the cheer. By working as a team we'd managed to finish everything pretty quickly.

"These pom-poms are awesome!" Sam exclaimed. She picked up two pom-poms and began waving them in the air. "Addie and her troops will pop their clogs when they see us with these."

"They'll what?" Chloe asked.

"Pop their clogs," Sam said. "You know, flip out."

I grinned and began shaking my pom-poms high. "Let the clog popping begin!" I exclaimed.

Chapter
TWO

I WAS TWO BLOCKS from the bus stop on Tuesday morning, and I'd already spotted Addie. She was hard to miss. After all, she was wearing a tall white hat with bright red stripes on it. It definitely caught my attention, which I'm sure was what she had in mind. The Pops love attention.

As I approached the corner, Addie turned and looked at the white baseball cap I was wearing. She shot me a triumphant smile. It was obvious she thought her hat was much cooler than mine. "Nice hat," she sneered sarcastically.

"Thanks." I pretended I didn't note the sarcasm in her voice. "Liza painted it herself . . . freehand."

Addie didn't seem impressed with my friend's artistic prowess. Apparently, she felt anything not created by a Pop wasn't worth her appreciation.

"Your hat's nice, too," I told her. "It's . . . um . . . really big."

"It is, isn't it?" Addie reached up and patted her head proudly. "My friends and I all went to the mall and picked them out together. When you have school spirit, you should show it off to everyone, don't you think?" She shot my little white baseball cap a pitiful glance. "Of course, that's just the way we see it. Everyone has their own way of showing their spirit, I guess."

I nodded and tried not to smile too broadly. After all, Addie had just given me a slam. It would seem weird for me to be happy about it. But I knew that I had a really big surprise hidden in my backpack.

The bus pulled up, and I grabbed a seat near the front. Addie took her usual seat — on the right near the middle. She always sat in the exact same spot, and she always sat by herself. Addie was the only Pop on our bus; and a Pop would never sit with a non-Pop. *Ever.* In fact, I was pretty sure that if the only seat left on the bus were next to one of us, Addie would climb up on the roof and ride to school up there.

Felicia got on at the next stop. As she sat down in the seat beside me, she turned around and smiled at Addie. "Nice hat," she complimented her, sounding only slightly sarcastic. "Where are Thing One and Thing Two?"

I giggled. Addie did look a little like the Cat in the Hat in that huge striped hat.

"You're so juvenile," Addie sighed. "Were Thing One and Thing Two characters in the book you were reading last night?"

"Ooo, slam!" Chip Lorimer shouted.

Addie smiled triumphantly for the second time that morning. Usually, a comment like that would've made me turn beet red with embarrassment (I'm a major blusher!), but Felicia didn't seem upset by it at all. Maybe that was because we both knew Addie would be totally freaked when she discovered what we'd planned!

She didn't have to wait long. Our bus was the last one to pull into the parking lot that morning, so the rest of my friends were already gathered together in a group. So were the Pops. They were all standing together in a big cluster near the brick wall, like they always did. From my seat high up on the bus, I got a good look at their hats. They looked like a Pop Peppermint Forest, kind of like the one on the Candy Land board game I had when I was a little kid.

"They think they're so cool," Felicia whispered to me. "But boy are they in for it!"

I wasn't sure why this whole school spirit thing had turned into a competition, I just knew that it had. Maybe it was because I was still kind of mad at Addie because she'd dumped me as a friend (but managed to keep my red T-shirt!). Or maybe it was because my friends and I were sick of the Pops trying to run our school. Either way, in the end, most things in our school wound up being competitions between the Pops and my friends. And this time, I knew for sure we were going to come out on top!

"Finally," Chloe huffed, as Felicia and I hurried over to where our friends were standing. "We've been waiting forever. The bell's going to ring any second."

"Sorry," I apologized. "We had to wait a while at the last stop."

"Mike Hoff have trouble getting out of bed in time for the bus again?" Josh asked.

Felicia and I nodded.

"I heard a great joke about an alarm clock . . ." Rachel began.

"Later," Sam said, stopping Rachel before she could finish her joke. "Right now, we have to cheer."

"I've got my camera ready," Marc told us. "This is going to be great."

"Be sure to get the faces of the Pops," Chloe told him. "They're going to freak."

Marc sighed. "I'm the director of this film," he reminded her. "I choose the angles I want to shoot."

One by one my friends and I dug into our backpacks and pulled out our pom-poms. The twins, Chloe, Felicia, Sam, and Rachel all seemed psyched. Liza, on the other hand, didn't look as anxious to cheer. I understood that. Liza wasn't the kind of person who liked drawing attention to herself. She was a behind-the-scenes type. I had a feeling she'd be more comfortable standing off to the side with Josh, watching us. But she'd already agreed to do our cheer with the rest of our *girl*friends.

"You okay?" I asked her.

Liza shrugged. "I'm not really into this sort of thing," she admitted quietly.

I nodded understandingly. "I know, but . . . well . . . someone has to show the Pops that they're not the only ones who care about our school. The Pops do so many mean things. They deserve to come in second once in a while, you know?"

Liza nodded. I knew she understood. Like the rest of us, she'd been the victim of the Pops' mean streak. They'd spread a horrible rumor about her cheating on the big history test. It wasn't true, but it made a lot of people suspicious, anyway. I hoped Liza could see that this was a way to show them up for a change. They deserved it!

"Okay," she said, taking a deep breath and fluffing up her pom-poms.

"Everyone ready?" Carolyn and Marilyn asked.

"Yeah!" we shouted back.

"Okay," Marc directed us. "Lights . . . camera . . . ACTION!"

And with that, we began waving our pom-poms in the air and cheering!

> *Joyce Kilmer Middle School!*
> *We're the kids who always rule!*
> *You know we have that super spirit.*
> *When we shout you really hear it.*
> *Other schools will hit the floor*
> *When they hear the lions ROAR!*

The shouting and applause from the other kids in the parking lot rang through my ears as we finished our cheer. It seemed like everyone was totally pumped up.

Well, *almost* everyone, anyway. There was complete silence coming from the Pop Peppermint Forest. They just stood there, with their eyes wide and their mouths open. They couldn't believe what my friends and I had come up with for Spirit Week. We'd totally beaten their Cat-in-the-Hat hat thing. My friends and I started cheering again. And this time everyone (but the Pops, of course) joined in.

> *Joyce Kilmer Middle School!*
> *We're the kids who always rule!*
> *You know we have that super spirit.*
> *When we shout you really hear it.*
> *Other schools will hit the floor,*
> *When they hear the lions ROAR!*

*   *   *

"That was legendary!" Rachel was still talking about our cheer three periods later as she, Sam, and I walked into science class together.

"Absolutely brill," Sam agreed.

"We'll definitely be going down in Joyce Kilmer Middle School history," I added.

At just that moment, Addie walked into the room. Her red-and-white hat had started to droop. So had her triumphant smile. She'd been beaten . . . badly. There was no way she'd be able to top what my friends and I had pulled off this morning. She knew it, and so did I. That's probably why she avoided my eyes completely as she sat down at a lab table next to Dana.

"Okay, everyone. I know you're all excited about Spirit Week, but we have some thrilling things going on in science right now, too," Mrs. Johnson said. "It's science fair time! I'm going to allow you all to choose your own partners. You don't have to choose someone in this class; your partner can be anyone in the sixth grade. After all, the sixth graders will all be given the same assignment rubric. I'm also not assigning topics. It's very open-ended."

I was glad I had so many friends who were seventh graders. I already knew all that. Chloe and I had decided last night that we were going to be partners for the science fair, even though we weren't in the same class. Good thing, too. Otherwise I might've felt bad when Rachel and Sam paired off to work together. I also knew Felicia and Josh had decided to do their project as a team — naturally. That way they could spend time together and do homework at the same time. Lucky Felicia — she had Mr. Wizard for a boyfriend *and* a science fair partner. That was going to be *some* project.

Of course, Addie and Dana were going to work together. I felt kind of bad for Addie, though. I hated to admit it, but Addie was really smart. Dana on the other hand . . . well . . . let's just say I had a feeling Addie would be doing a lot of the work on her own. But I knew Addie would rather do all the work than have to spend time working outside of school with a non-Pop. Not that I would have wanted to be her partner or anything. Although if this had been the old days, she and I definitely would've paired off. But this wasn't the old days, and that wasn't happening.

Which was fine, actually, since Chloe would be a lot more fun to work with, no matter what project we picked. Right now, we had no idea what kind of experiment we were going to do. But we were getting together at my house after school to brainstorm ideas. I figured between the two of us we could come up with something really awesome. Something we could really *cheer* about!

I met up with Chloe on the way to the cafeteria for lunch. She was still carrying her pom-poms. "Where are yours?" she asked me.

"I stuffed them in my locker," I explained. "I had too many books to carry."

"That's okay," Chloe said, handing me one of her white pom-poms. "We can share." I grinned and waved the pom-pom in the air as we entered the cafeteria.

"What kind of slop do you think they're serving today?" Chloe wondered.

I glanced down at people's trays to see what today's red-and-white lunch was. Spaghetti and tomato sauce, red Jell-O, and whipped cream. Not bad. Although I was pretty sure the spaghetti would be overcooked and the whipped cream would be flavorless. Still, they had served worse stuff before. I picked up a tray and got into the food line with Chloe.

"Nice cheer this morning." Sandee Wind, the eighth grade class president congratulated us. "And the pom-poms are cool."

"Thanks," I said happily. Sandee and I were both on the student council — I was the sixth grade class president — but she rarely spoke to me outside of student council meetings. It was pretty impressive that she was complimenting me in front of her eighth grade friends. "My friends and I really wanted to show our school spirit."

"You did," Sandee assured me. "More than anyone."

More than anyone, I repeated silently to myself. Which meant more than the Pops. I stood a little taller, proud that my friends and I were the most spirited people in all of Joyce Kilmer Middle School.

Or were we? At that very moment, Addie, Sabrina, Claire, and Dana strolled into the cafeteria. Everyone stared at them. And it wasn't because they were wearing cool hats. Nor was it because they were Pops. They had all painted red-and-white flowers on their faces!

"Whoa! Check them out," Sandee exclaimed, turning her attention from Chloe and me to the Pops. "They must've used up an entire lipstick making those flowers."

I sighed. I should've known better than to underestimate Addie and her friends. They'd pooled their white eye shadow and red lipstick and somehow managed to grab the school's attention back from us.

Now it was *my* turn to droop a little. And as I sat down at our table, I could tell my pals all felt the same way I did.

"You have to admit, that's an artistic use of lipstick," Liza said with a sigh.

"I hope they all break out in spots," Sam groaned.

"Spots?" I asked.

"You know, *zits*," Sam explained. "A girl could really clog her pores wearing all that makeup."

Chloe shook her head. "It will never happen," she said. "Even zits don't want to get that close to the Pops."

"Well, they beat us once again," I said, looking over at where Addie, Claire, Dana, and Sabrina were sitting. Triumphant smiles had returned to their faces.

"I wonder where Maya is," Marc said. "She's never far from the rest of them. She must be doing something *really* incredible."

"More incredible than that?" I asked. "What could that be?"

"Oh, plenty of things," Josh butted in. "Ideas are infinite. Imagine if someone had said there was nothing more incredible than the computer, and we never got the Internet."

I sighed. Usually I found Josh pretty fascinating. But today I wasn't in the mood for his words of wisdom. Besides, he was right. Because at that moment, something even more spirited than painted faces and Cat-in-the-Hat hats entered the room.

"Whoa! Check it out!" Marc exclaimed.

"It's a lion!" Carolyn exclaimed.

"A mascot," Marilyn added.

The twins were right. There was a lion in our cafeteria. Not a real one, of course. It was a person in a lion costume, like something you'd see at Disneyland or Six Flags. Except this lion costume looked kind of ratty. Some of the fur was missing from its body, and one ear was sort of flopping to the side. The costume looked really old.

"I didn't know we had a mascot," I said.

"We didn't," Carolyn told me.

"Until now," Marilyn noted.

"I wonder who's in there," Sam said.

"It's either a short teacher or a kid. The costume's only big enough to fit someone about five foot one or two," Josh pointed out.

"I think it's kind of babyish," Marilyn said.

"Like something you'd have in the cafeteria in elementary school," Carolyn agreed.

"I think it's kind of cool," Liza countered, "in a weird sort of way."

I didn't know what to think. The mascot was babyish *and* cool — if it was possible to be both at the same time. And I could tell most people in the cafeteria felt the same way. They couldn't tell whether the lion mascot was a great way to show school spirit, or something that was just silly. There was a buzz going through the room, as everyone tried to figure out where they stood on the issue.

And then, suddenly, I heard some really loud shouting coming from across the room — at the *Pops' table*.

"It's Maya!" I heard Sabrina shout. "It's got to be!"

"That's why she's not here!" Dana exclaimed.

I looked over at their table. Addie was sitting there, staring at the costumed lion. From her expression, I could tell she was as surprised by the appearance of our school mascot as anyone. And Addie did *not* like to be surprised. But what she liked less was letting other people know she'd been caught by surprise.

So *I* was not surprised when Addie burst into applause as the lion passed by her table. "Go Maya!" she shouted excitedly.

As soon as Addie began clapping, everyone else in the cafeteria did, too. It was as though once the Pops had given the school mascot a seal of approval, it was okay for everyone else to think it was cool.

I watched as Marc pulled out his camera and began filming the action in the cafeteria. He was focusing more on the way the kids were cheering than on the lion itself. I thought that was kind of strange, since I figured the lion was the whole point. But then again, I'm not a filmmaker, and Marc is. He must've known what he was doing.

"Do you really think that's Maya in there?" I asked Josh.

"I have no idea," he said with a shrug.

I laughed. I think that was the first time I'd ever heard my genius friend say those four words.

Chloe was still griping about the lion mascot later that afternoon, as she and I sat in my bedroom trying to come up with an idea for our science fair experiment. "I can't believe how far the Pops will go to get attention," she moaned.

"I know," I agreed. "But you have to admit that mascot costume was pretty amazing. I wonder where they found it."

"*I* wonder how they convinced Maya to wear it," Chloe said. "It's not exactly typical Pop fashion."

"That's true." I laughed. "Of course, now that one of them has worn it, we'll probably see everyone wearing lion costumes tomorrow."

Chloe rolled her eyes. She knew what I meant. The Pops could set any trend, no matter how ridiculous.

Just then, my mice, Sam and Cody, began to squeak. I walked over to the dresser and lifted Sam out of the cage, handing him a treat. I put another treat in the cage for Cody. "This way they won't fight," I explained, as I held Sam in my hand and watched him eat.

Chloe nodded, and began studying the science book I'd left open on the bed intently.

"You want to hold Cody?" I asked her.

"Um . . . no thanks," Chloe replied.

"You sure? He's awfully soft."

Chloe shook her head. "It's okay. We should really get going on this project."

That was weird. Usually, I was the one who had to put Chloe back on track when it came to homework. She was usually the procrastination queen! But not today. And she was right. Mrs. Johnson would be expecting our proposal for our experiment tomorrow morning.

I sat down on the bed beside her. "So what do you want to work on?" I asked.

Chloe gave me a funny look. "Do you . . . um . . . think you could put that back in the cage?" She glanced quickly at Sam and then looked away.

"What? Sam?" I asked.

Chloe nodded. She gave me another look. "I wonder how our friend Sam feels about sharing a name with a mouse."

"She loves it," I assured her. "She thinks it's hilarious. She's really into pets. She had to leave her ferret, Francine, with a friend when she moved here from England." I giggled. "Francine Ferret with a friend. Say that five times fast."

But Chloe wasn't laughing. "Do you think you could put *that* Sam back in his cage so we can get started?" she asked me.

"Sure," I agreed. Then I placed my mouse back in his house. He scampered immediately over to his wheel and started running around and around.

Chloe sighed. "That squeaking is going to make me crazy. Maybe we should work downstairs in your living room or something."

I studied Chloe's face. She looked upset. "You don't like my mice, do you?" I asked her.

Chloe kind of scrunched her mouth up a little bit and frowned. "It's nothing personal against them," she told me. "It's just that, well . . . I don't like *any* mice. They freak me out with those beady eyes. . . ."

"My mice do *not* have beady eyes!" I exclaimed. "They have adorable eyes."

"And their long, skinny tails," Chloe continued. "Those are really creepy, Jen."

I was about to defend Sam and Cody's tails the way I had their eyes, but I stopped myself. Chloe wasn't the first person I'd met who was scared of mice. Lots of people were. I thought that was ridiculous because mice — especially *my* mice — were really sweet once you got to know them. "I wish you'd give Sam and Cody a chance, Chloe," I said gently. "They're not scary at all. They're soft and cuddly. The truth is, they're probably more scared of you than you are of them."

"I doubt that," Chloe insisted. She refused to even look in the direction of the cage.

"How come you never told me this before?" I asked Chloe.

"You never actually took either of them out of the cage before while I was over," Chloe explained. "As long as they stayed over there, and I stayed over here . . ." Her voice drifted off uncomfortably.

"We can go downstairs," I said slowly.

"Good!" Chloe exclaimed happily.

"But then you'd be afraid of my mice forever," I continued. "And that's not cool."

"It's no big deal," Chloe assured me.

"Yeah, it is," I told her. "Because then every time you come over here, I'll feel like we can't hang out in my room."

"I didn't say that," Chloe replied. "Like I told you. As long as they stay in their cage . . ."

"But I would always feel bad," I said. "And you'd be missing out, because Sam and Cody are great pets." I stopped for a minute and thought. "Maybe if you spent some time with them you could see that."

Chloe frowned. "I don't like the sound of this."

"I wish I could train you to like mice," I continued. "A little at a time. Like today, you could just stay here in the same room with them. And then next time, you could sit in a chair near their cage and . . ."

Chloe shook her head. "You want to train me?" she asked. "You train *animals*, Jen. Not people. What, are you going to give me a treat every time I sit up or roll over?"

Now I felt bad. Chloe sounded angry. I hadn't meant to hurt her feelings or anything. I'd only been trying to help her get over her fear of mice.

"Besides, I think I came over here to work on a science fair project, not to *be* a science fair project," Chloe continued.

"That's it!" I exclaimed excitedly. "I've got it."

Chloe looked at me strangely. "You've got what?"

"Our science fair project," I told her. "Your fear of mice gave me the greatest idea."

"*I'm* going to be our science fair project?" Chloe sounded very confused.

I shook my head. "No. Sam and Cody are going to be our science fair project. We're going to train them to run through mazes."

"Uh-uh!" Chloe shook her head. "No way. I'm not going to work with mice for our project."

"But it would be great for you," I told her. "You'd get to know them and you wouldn't be afraid of mice anymore. And I think we'd get an A. Teachers love when you use live animals in an experiment."

Actually, I had no idea what teachers liked to see when you did a middle school science project. I'd never done one before. But one thing I was sure of was that the idea of getting an A on the science fair project would catch Chloe's attention. Science is her worst subject. She'd gotten a C-minus on our rocks and minerals unit test. She needed an A on this project.

"You think we'd get an A? Really?" she asked.

See? I nodded. "Totally. We could build a twisty-turny maze for each of them out of wood. Then we could put sugar water at the end of Sam's maze, and regular water at the end of Cody's. We could test how having a sweet reward affects the learning process in mice."

Chloe seemed really impressed. Actually, I was really impressed myself. I don't know where I got that whole affects-the-learning-process thing. I must have heard it somewhere. Maybe on TV or in a movie. I knew I'd never read it anywhere. I wasn't all that into reading science books.

"Well . . ." Chloe started out slowly. "I guess if I didn't actually have to touch the mice . . ."

"Oh, I'll do that part," I said. "You can build the mazes and type up the lab report."

"I can do that," Chloe agreed. "I'm actually pretty good at writing lab reports."

I smiled. "And if at some point you actually feel like holding Sam or Cody, you can," I suggested.

Chloe shivered slightly. "I don't think that's going to happen," she told me. She glanced at the cage quickly. "What do you say we go use your *downstairs* computer to type up our proposal?"

I shrugged. "Sure."

Chloe grabbed her notebook and hurried out of the room. I followed behind. Before I left, I turned toward Cody and Sam's cage. "Don't worry, guys," I told the mice. "She'll get to love you."

"Don't bet on it," Chloe called back from the staircase. "It's never going to happen."

Chapter
THREE

I'D BEEN LOOKING FORWARD to Wednesday of Spirit Week. It was Wacky Dress-up Day, and for once I figured I wouldn't be out-fashioned by the Pops. After all, the whole point of the day was to look as bizarre as possible.

So I was feeling pretty confident as I walked to the bus stop. I was wearing the red, white, purple, and green tie-dye shirt that I'd made at overnight camp last summer. I'd matched my shirt with a blue-and-green paisley print skirt (well, actually, it *didn't* match, which was the point). My purple Converse sneakers finished off the look. There was no way anyone would look wackier than me.

But as I approached the bus stop, I could see I was wrong. Not only had Addie gone wackier with her clothes, but somehow she'd managed to look pretty chic in her out-fit. Addie was wearing a black shirt with red polka dots and black-and-red striped tights, but the wacky parts were the black-and-silver wings Addie had attached to her back, and the headband with red antennae she was wearing on her head. Addie had decided to dress like a ladybug for Wacky Dress-up Day. She'd come in costume! Now why hadn't I thought of that?

Because I'm not Addie Wilson, I groaned to myself. And

it was the truth. No one else could've come up with an outfit like that and made it work. Addie just had an eye for putting things together. She never looked out of place or inappropriate. But she always looked better than everyone else.

I glanced down at my outfit. Suddenly, the tie-dye colors didn't seem as bright. I just paled in comparison to Addie – again. *Grrrrr.*

I felt a little better when the bus came to Felicia's stop. She hadn't thought to make a costume out of her wacky clothes, either. She'd just put on a lot of stuff that didn't match. And as our bus pulled into the school parking lot, I could tell everyone – even the other Pops – had done exactly what we had.

It was kind of funny seeing Sabrina, Claire, Dana, and Maya all dressed in absolutely hideous outfits. Dana's was especially ugly – she was wearing a purple sequined sleeveless shirt with red yoga pants and lemon-yellow platform shoes. The shoes were really high, and she was towering over all the other Pops.

Not to be outdone, my friends had come up with some pretty bizarre outfits. Josh was wearing a blue button-down shirt – which he'd buttoned wrong – and a pair of khakis. He had a tie around his neck that was dotted with neon green frogs, which matched the neon green flip-flops on his feet.

But Josh was nothing compared to Sam. She was wearing a blue wig that was so bright you could see it from miles away. The wig matched the stripes in her blue-and-white striped leggings, which she'd paired with a hot pink-and-yellow checked shirt.

"You guys look great!" Liza said, as she came running over to us in a pair of overall shorts she'd decorated with what seemed to be hundreds of iron-on patches.

"You look pretty wonky yourself," Sam complimented her.

"That's *wacky*, not wonky," Chloe corrected her.

Sam blushed slightly. "Right. Wacky. Sorry," she apologized.

Chloe laughed. "You can take the girl out of England but you can't take the England out of the girl," she teased.

"I like your shirt," I said, admiring Chloe's bubblegum pink tee. It read More Candy, Less War.

"And don't you love the way the pink *doesn't* match my red gauchos?" Chloe asked me.

"Perfect," I told her. I turned to the twins. "How long did it take you guys to come up with those outfits?" I asked them.

Marilyn and Carolyn spun around so we could get a better view of their matching black, purple, and pink paisley skirts, which they'd paired with T-shirts that had pictures of trout and flounders all over them.

"Not long," Marilyn said.

"The hardest part was finding two of these shirts," Carolyn added.

"It's hard to believe anyone made more than one," Rachel said.

"I like them," Chloe said.

That didn't come as a surprise to any of us.

"Hey, look," Felicia said, pointing to the parking lot stairs. "Here comes Maya again." Sure enough, the lion mascot was leaving the school building.

I shook my head. "That's not Maya," I told her. "She's over there with the Pops. See? She's wearing rolled-up jeans and rainbow suspenders."

"Then who's inside the costume?" Felicia wondered.

Everyone else seemed to be wondering the same thing. I could tell they were looking around, checking out who was in the parking lot and who wasn't.

"Hey, where's Marc?" Chloe asked suddenly.

"I don't know," I answered her. "Maybe he's sick or something. Was he on the bus with you?"

Chloe nodded. "Yeah, I sat next to him. We talked the whole way here. He'd be hard to miss – he's wearing a bright orange-and-yellow Hawaiian shirt." She glanced around the parking lot, searching for Marc's shirt. "One minute he was here, and the next he was gone."

Hmmm . . . Was it possible that Marc was inside the mascot costume? I thought about that for a minute. It was hard to imagine my friend walking around the school parking lot inside a lion suit. It just wasn't his style. Marc wasn't exactly Mr. School Spirit. In fact, he was rarely involved in anything school-related, with the exception of the film club. When it came to school, Marc was more of an observer than a participant — carrying around his camera and catching what everyone *else* was doing on film. Besides, Marc had been the one filming the lion in the cafeteria yesterday, so it couldn't be him.

But if it wasn't Marc — and it certainly wasn't Maya — who *was* in the lion suit? On first glance, no one else seemed to be missing from any of the other groups around the school.

Most importantly, everyone could tell that the person in the suit wasn't one of the Pops. They were all present and accounted for. And that definitely put a whole different spin on things. Without any cheering or excitement coming from the Pops' corner, no one seemed particularly interested in the lion. In fact, they just kind of ignored the faded, tattered mascot completely.

Actually, there wasn't much time to think about the mascot, or anything else for that matter. A moment later, the first bell rang. It was time to get to class.

"Okay, class, put your books under your chairs and take out your pencils," my teacher, Ms. Jaffe, announced as I got settled into my first period English class. "We're going to have a quiz on the literary terms we learned yesterday."

"A quiz?" Dana Harrison moaned. "But you didn't say anything about a quiz. You didn't even give us homework last night."

"It's a pop quiz, Dana," Ms. Jaffe explained, as she calmly handed out the papers.

You would think someone like Dana, who was a Pop, would do well on a pop quiz. But from the look on her face, I could tell that wasn't going to happen. Those were two completely different kinds of pops. (Oh, and btw, I knew the literary term for the double meaning of pop, too. Words that are spelled and pronounced the same way but have different meanings are called homonyms! Maybe that would be on the quiz.)

I glanced over at Sam and Chloe to get their reactions to the pop quiz. Sam looked pretty calm — no surprise there. She always did really well in English, and Ms. Jaffe almost always gave her A's.

But Chloe had a look of absolute terror on her face. I felt bad for her. She definitely didn't look ready for a quiz. She probably hadn't discovered the unwritten rule I'd figured out after being faced with pop quizzes in some of my other classes.

MIDDLE SCHOOL RULE # 27:

IF YOU DON'T HAVE ANY HOMEWORK ONE NIGHT, LOOK OVER YOUR NOTES INSTEAD. NOT HAVING ANY HOMEWORK IS A CLUE THAT YOU COULD HAVE A SURPRISE QUIZ THE NEXT DAY. TEACHERS ARE SNEAKY THAT WAY.

I was certainly glad I'd spent ten minutes going over the literary terms we'd learned in class the day before. I looked down at the first question.

Which of the following is a simile?

A. The sky was as blue as the sea.

B. The doll's eyes followed me around the room.

C. Peter Piper picked a peck of pickled peppers.

As I circled letter A, I smiled to myself. Apparently middleschoolsurvival.com quizzes weren't the only ones I was good at taking.

I'd practically forgotten about the English quiz by the time I got to my fifth period lunch, but Chloe was still moaning about it. "Why do I have to know what alliteration is, anyway? What am I going to do with that?"

"You'd be surprised," Sam said. "It can be really effective when you're writing a *perfectly persuasive paper*."

Chloe rolled her eyes and took a bite of her pizza. I could tell she didn't feel like arguing about this with Sam. So I changed the subject.

"You're coming over to work on our science project today, aren't you?" I asked Chloe.

Chloe nodded. "Yeah. Only don't make me think about it while I'm eating."

"Are you guys doing something really gross?" Liza asked us.

"No," I told her.

"Yes," Chloe answered at the same time.

Carolyn and Marilyn both started to giggle. "You guys sound like us," Marilyn said.

"Except in reverse," Carolyn added.

I knew what they meant. The twins often spoke at the same time. But they were always in agreement. Chloe and me? Not so much. At least not right now, anyway. I glared at her. "They are not gross," I said, defending my mice.

"Well, don't tell me what you're doing," Liza told us. "The best thing about the science fair is being surprised at what your friends have been working on."

"I'll bet you and Felicia are going to do something amazing," I told Josh.

"Oh, we are," he said proudly. "It's going to blow you away."

Just then, Marc walked over to the table and sat down in the chair beside me. "Hey, guys, what's up?" he asked us.

"You've changed your clothes since this morning," Chloe told him.

"Huh?" Marc looked down at his wild Hawaiian shirt. "No I haven't. I was wearing this. You saw me on the bus."

"But we didn't see you in the parking lot a few minutes later," Chloe told him knowingly. "Or *did* we?"

"What're you talking about?" Marc asked.

"She's talking about your amazing disappearing act this morning," Sam explained. "One minute you're getting off the bus, the next minute you're nowhere to be found."

Marc looked at her curiously.

"We just want to know," Liza said slowly. "Was that you in the lion suit?"

Marc frowned. "I thought that was Maya," he said.

"So did we," Carolyn told him.

"But she was in the parking lot today when the lion appeared again," Marilyn added.

"Well, I was here with you guys yesterday at lunch when the lion came to the cafeteria," Marc reminded them.

That was true, he was. But it still didn't explain this morning. Which apparently was what Josh was thinking as well. "So where were you before school today?" he asked Marc.

"I was doing something for Mrs. Arlington," Marc explained. "There was a science DVD thing she needed help with."

Well, that made sense. I knew the kids in the film class often helped out the teachers with stuff like DVD players. Our teachers were pretty smart about the subjects they taught, but they weren't always so brilliant when it came to electronics.

Everyone else seemed satisfied with his answer, too. At least they were done giving him the third degree. And I was glad. I didn't feel like dealing with any hostility right now. I had a feeling I'd be getting a lot of that from Chloe this afternoon when we started working on our science fair project.

Chapter
FOUR

TURNS OUT I WAS RIGHT. Chloe started moaning and groaning the second I opened the front door of my house. "Do we have to go up to your room right now?" she asked me. "Can't we start building the mazes down here? You can bring the mice down later . . . *after I've gone home.*"

I shook my head. "That's not the way we planned to do it," I reminded her. "We were going to work on everything together."

"You said I didn't have to touch the mice," Chloe said. "At least not right away. I have to build up to that."

"But you're not going to build up to anything if you stay down here," I said.

"That's okay with me," Chloe replied.

"You know, it's kind of insulting that you don't like my mice," I told her.

"Why?" Chloe asked. "I didn't say I didn't like *you.*"

"But they're *my* pets." I studied Chloe's face. Clearly, she wasn't getting it. "Maybe you don't understand because you don't have any pets," I told her.

"Rub it in why don't you?" Chloe growled at me.

Now I felt bad. I knew Chloe had been bugging her parents for a pet for months. But her dad had just gotten a new job after having been out of work for a while, and her folks had said that any extra expense or responsibility would be too much right now.

I really hadn't meant to hurt Chloe's feelings. I was just upset because she'd been dissing my mice. And because she wasn't being a very good partner. "We're supposed to be a team, Chloe," I explained. "And you are *so* not being a team player."

"I am, too!"

"You are not!"

"Yes I am," Chloe repeated.

"Then prove it," I insisted. "Come upstairs with me to see the mice."

Chloe turned white at the idea of it. "There has to be another way," she insisted.

"I don't know of any," I said.

"I do," Chloe insisted. "I could take a quiz on middleschoolsurvival.com."

"We don't even know if there's a quiz about being a team player on the site," I told her.

"I'm sure there is. They have quizzes about everything," Chloe pointed out.

And she was right. A few minutes later, Chloe and I were sitting in front of my downstairs computer answering questions.

There's No "I" in Team!

How do you handle a group effort? There's only one way to find out if you're a true team player. You've got to take this quiz. And by the way, this isn't a team effort. You have to answer the questions on your own.

1. **It's your little brother's birthday, and he wants to go out for all-you-can-eat sushi. You are not in the mood for raw fish and rice. What's your reaction?**

   A. You go along and order up roll after roll of tuna, rice, and eel. After all, it's his b-day!
   B. You go, but you refuse to eat.
   C. You tell your parents you refuse to be part of the celebration unless they choose a place you feel like going to.

   Chloe thought about that one for a moment. "I'm not really a raw fish person," she admitted. "It's so slimy."

   "I don't think the food's the point of the question, Chloe," I told her. "It's more how you react to the situation."

   "I guess I'd choose B," Chloe said finally. "I just can't imagine myself eating that junk."

I nodded and clicked on the letter B. The screen immediately changed to the next question.

2. **Your class is doing geography projects. Your group has been assigned France. Someone has to store all the boxes you'll be using to build the Eiffel Tower. As you're the only one in the group who doesn't share a room with a sibling, your space is a natural for storage. What do you tell the others?**

   A. Your cousin is staying with you this week, so you have nowhere to put the boxes.
   B. Sure. No prob. Just bring the boxes over.
   C. You agree to store half of the boxes, but not all. You shouldn't have to give up all your living space.

"B again," Chloe said, sounding far more definite this time. "I was going to suggest we build the mazes at my house, anyway."

I was pretty sure that was Chloe's way of getting away from my mice for part of the project, but I didn't say that. I just clicked on the letter B and waited for the computer to flash the next quiz question.

3. **You've been watching a modeling competition show all season long. Tonight's the big finale. But, the coach of your softball team has planned an extra practice so your team will be ready for the big game tomorrow. What do you do?**

A. Go to practice but say you have to leave early. That way you can at least catch the end of the show.
B. Call your coach and cough into the phone. You're too sick for practice, but you're sure you'll be fine tomorrow.
C. Go to the practice, and ask your mom to TiVo the show. You'll just have to wait to find out who the winner is.

"C," Chloe said without even taking a moment to think about it. "I missed a lot of my favorite shows when I was rehearsing the school play. And we don't even have TiVo."

I clicked "C." "Okay, here's the next one."

4. Your English teacher is allowing you to choose two other kids to act out a scene from <u>A Midsummer Night's Dream</u>. How do you decide which two thespians you want to perform with you?

A. You choose two kids who can't act their way out of a paper bag, so you'll look better.
B. You choose the lead from the school play and give her the biggest part. She's bound to make you all look good.
C. Ask your two BFFs to do the scene with you. None of you are exactly Oscar-winning actresses, but at least you'll all have a good time during your rehearsals.

Chloe thought about that one for a while. I could tell that something in the question was upsetting her.

"A," she said finally. "I know that makes me sound like a jerk. But when I'm on stage, I really like to stand out."

Chloe actually likes to stand out no matter where she is. But I didn't say that. It was obviously pretty difficult for her to admit how she really felt. I didn't want to make it worse. "Okay, here's number five," I said instead.

5. You're the starting center forward on your school soccer team. But the coach wants to give everyone a chance to play. How do you react to being benched?

A. Accept the coach's decision gracefully, and stick around to cheer on the team.

B. Shout out instructions to the second string. After all, they're sure to benefit from your experience — and you don't want to lose the lead you've gotten for them.

C. Leave. You've done your job.

"I always try to have team spirit," Chloe said slowly, as she looked over her options on the screen. "But I do kind of like to have a little control over things."

A *little* control? I bit my lip and tried hard not to laugh. Chloe could be a real control freak when she wanted to be.

I guess she realized that, because she finally answered, "B. Make it B. I would want to be sure that the team still won, even if I wasn't actually playing."

Chloe knew herself really well. I clicked the letter B and waited for the screen to change. A moment later, a message popped up.

So are you a team player or solo superstar? Add up your points!

1. A) 3   B) 2   C) 1
2. A) 1   B) 3   C) 2
3. A) 2   B) 1   C) 3
4. A) 1   B) 2   C) 3
5. A) 3   B) 2   C) 1

You scored 11 points. Now find out what that says about you:

12-15 points: Wow! Team is your middle name. You give your all to any group project. Just make sure your other team members don't take advantage of your generous spirit.

8-11 points: You can adjust to being part of a team, but it's not your favorite way to work. You can always be counted on to complete your assignments, but you're not one to volunteer for any extra duty.

5-7 points: Teamwork? No way! You're better off solo. Sharing the spotlight — and the workload — is not your greatest strength. Still, you're going to have to learn to adjust. Sometimes there's no escaping the dreaded group assignment!

Chloe sat there for a moment, reading the results to herself. Finally, she said, "I thought I would score higher."

"You scored pretty high," I assured her. "You're at the

top of the middle section. That means you're a team player more often than you're not."

"But I wish I'd done better," Chloe told me.

"Well, you could change your score," I said.

"You mean take the quiz again?" Chloe asked. "The score would only change if I lied about some of my answers. And what would the point of that be?"

"I didn't mean that," I explained. "I just meant you could try harder to be more of a team player."

"How?" Chloe asked.

"Well, you could start by coming upstairs and working in the same room as Sam and Cody," I suggested. "You don't have to hold them or anything. At least not today."

Chloe frowned. She opened her mouth to say something but stopped suddenly. Then she took a deep breath. "Okay, teammate," she said in a less than enthusiastic voice. "Let's go see the little critters."

"Cool," I said, as I started for the stairs. Chloe followed close behind, but didn't say anything. I figured she was really nervous.

I know people are freaked out by mice. You see it all the time in cartoons — women jumping on tables and stuff as a mouse runs by. But those are field mice — and they're usually uninvited dirty guests who leave gross droppings all over the place. My mice are different. They're snow white, and they live in a cage — which I clean nearly every day. There was no reason for Chloe to be scared of them.

"My dad picked up a lot of pieces of wood and strong

glue for us to use for the mazes," I said, jabbering on as we entered my room so that Chloe wouldn't have time to focus on being nervous about the mice. "I think we should build the two mazes so they're identical. That's the only way we can be sure we're testing the whole reward thing. If one maze is harder than the other, it won't work."

Chloe nodded. She sat down on my floor next to the pile of wood and pulled out her notebook. "I actually sketched out a few ideas for mazes," she said. "Nothing too tough. Just enough turns to keep it challenging."

"Great!" I exclaimed happily. "I'm so glad you did that. That'll save us a lot of time."

"See," Chloe insisted. "I *am* a team player."

I frowned slightly. Chloe was still upset about the results of that quiz. But she hadn't really done that badly. "Okay, teammate," I said, "let's get building."

Two hours later, we had built two nice looking, identical wooden mazes. There were little gates at the start, and water at the end of each one. There was sugar water in Sam's bottle, and regular water in Cody's.

"Okay, it's time to let the mice run their first race," I said. I went over to my desk and pulled out a clean pad of paper. Then I used a ruler to draw a line down the center of the page to make two columns. I marked one column SAM and the other CODY. "You keep track of how long it takes each mouse to run," I told Chloe.

Chloe nodded and took a deep breath. I knew she was nervous about looking at the mice while they raced. She'd been avoiding looking over at the cage up until now. Still, she was definitely happy that I was the one who was going to be taking the mice out of their cages and putting them in the maze.

"Okay, Sam, here's your maze," I said, as I placed one of my pet mice behind his starting gate. "And, Cody, this one's yours."

"How can you tell them apart?" Chloe asked. "They're both white mice."

"Easy. Cody has a little brown dot in the middle of his tail," I told her.

Chloe glanced at Cody just long enough to spot the dot. "I really hate those tails," she murmured. Then she stopped herself. "No offense," she added.

"It's okay," I said, giving her a smile. I knew she was trying to be brave about being around the mice.

"I brought my good watch, the one with the second hand," Chloe told me. "That way we can know exactly how long it takes each mouse to finish his maze."

"Okay," I agreed. Then I looked down at the mice. "Go!" I said, opening the gates of both mazes at exactly the same time.

I watched as Sam and Cody made their way through their mazes, getting confused at certain stops, then turning around, and eventually reaching the end. Cody finished a few seconds before Sam, which seemed weird, since it was Sam who had the sugar water at the end of his maze. Of course, he didn't know that until after he'd tasted it, and I figured that had to have affected things. "How fast did they do that?" I asked Chloe.

"Well, Cody finished in sixty-three seconds," Chloe told me. "But I didn't get a chance to get Sam's time because I was writing down Cody's."

Hmmm. That was going to be a problem. "I think I should write down Sam's times, and you should do Cody's from now on," I told Chloe. "Otherwise we're never going to be able to get accurate times. And you know how into accuracy Mrs. Johnson is."

Chloe nodded. "Accuracy is the building block of science," she said, pursing her lips slightly and imitating Ms. Johnson's clipped teacher voice. I giggled. Chloe can really be hilarious when she wants to be. She imitates every teacher in the school perfectly. I opened my desk drawer and pulled out my pink-and-purple watch, which had a second hand that could be used for timing the race. Then I picked up Sam and Cody and placed them back at the beginnings of their mazes.

"Let's try it again, okay?" I asked them. The mice squeaked. It wasn't actually a reply, but I figured it could count as one.

"On your marks, get set, go!" I shouted as I lifted the gates and sent the mice on their way again. This time, Sam beat Cody by four seconds.

"One more time," Chloe said. "Best out of three."

"Okay," I agreed. "But then we should give them a rest."

"Agreed."

I placed the mice at their starting gates. "On your marks, get set, go!" I shouted as I opened the gates.

Once again the mice began running through their mazes. But this time, something really weird happened. Chloe started cheering. "Go Cody! Go Cody!" she exclaimed. "No. Not that way. Turn around. Yeah that's it!"

I looked at her with surprise. Talk about competitive. Of course, I can be pretty competitive when I want to be, too. "Go Sam!" I shouted back. "You can do it!"

A few seconds later, Sam and Cody were both happily drinking from their water bottles. And once again, Sam had been the winner.

"Well, it's not exactly fair," Chloe told me. "I mean Sam *is* the one with the sugar in his water. So of course he's more motivated to reach the end of the maze first."

"That's the whole point of the experiment, Chloe," I reminded her.

"I know," Chloe told me. "I'm just saying . . ." She reached down and tentatively pet Cody on the back. "You would have won if it had been fair," she told him. Then she looked up at me, surprised. "He *is* really soft."

"I told you." I smiled. Sam wasn't the only one who had learned something new really quickly. "We should get them back in their cages," I told Chloe, as I picked up Sam and rested him in my palm. I cupped my other hand over him so he couldn't get loose. "You want to get Cody?"

Chloe wrinkled her nose. "No. I don't want to feel him squirming around in my hand . . . at least not yet."

I nodded. I wasn't going to push it. Chloe had made enough progress for one day.

"Tomorrow we'll build a different maze," I told her, as I put Cody back in the cage with Sam. "But this time Cody will get the sugar water. If Cody wins in the new maze, then we know it's the sugar. If Sam wins again, it'll probably mean he's just faster."

"Oh, Cody will win," Chloe assured me. "He's smart."

"So is Sam," I said.

"But not as smart as Cody. I can tell."

I laughed. Suddenly, Chloe was acting as though Cody was *her* mouse, and she was determined to have him win at any cost. Pretty funny, considering that less than two hours ago she couldn't even bear to look at his tail. "You crack me up," I told my friend.

"Why?" Chloe asked. From the expression on her face I could tell she genuinely had no idea what was so funny. But I kept my mouth shut. This was probably the first time Chloe had ever felt this proud of an animal. And I didn't want to do anything that might break up the *team* of Chloe and Cody.

My cell phone rang later that night. It was Chloe. "Hey, what's up?" I asked her.

"You're not going to believe this!" Chloe exclaimed. "The most wonderful, incredible thing happened on my way home from your house today. Honestly, Jen, you'll never believe it."

"How do you know unless you tell me what this wonderful, incredible thing is?" I teased her.

"Well, I was walking home from your house and . . ." Chloe began. She stopped for a minute, and I could swear I heard a dog barking in the background.

"Where are you?" I asked her.

"In my house," Chloe said.

"But there's a dog . . ." I started.

"That's the incredible thing!" Chloe exclaimed. "I got a dog!"

"When . . . how . . . ?"

"He followed me home from your house," Chloe said.

"Whose dog is he?" I asked.

"I don't know," Chloe explained. "He didn't have any tags or anything. He was lost."

"And your mom let you keep him?" I wondered excitedly.

"She said just until we find out who he belongs to," Chloe told me. "She thinks someone will put an ad in the paper or something. But I don't think that's going to happen. It looks like he's been missing for a while. He was pretty dirty and hungry when I found him."

"This is so cool!" I exclaimed excitedly. "Have you given him a name yet?"

"I'm calling him Bud," Chloe said.

"Bud," I repeated the name out loud. "I like that. It's so friendly."

"I know. My parents like the name, too," Chloe told me. "And so does Bud. Every time I say it, he wags his tail."

"That's a sure sign," I agreed.

"He's so cute, Jen," Chloe gushed. "He's got all this wiry gray and white fur. His left ear stands straight up, but his right ear bends a little at the top. And his eyes are so brown. When he looks at me, I just melt."

"He sounds adorable."

"He is. He really is. Right now he's sitting right up against me. I can feel his little heart beating."

"So when can I come over to meet him?" I asked her.

"How about after school tomorrow?" Chloe asked me. "We can play with him for a while and then go to your house to do our science experiment with *your* pets."

I smiled. Chloe was obviously really happy to have joined the world of pet owners. And I was happy for her. Now she would understand the special bond I have with Cody and Sam. I had a feeling I would never have to worry about her saying mean things about my mice ever again.

Chapter

FIVE

CHLOE WAS ALL SMILES when she arrived at school Thursday morning. "Hi!" she exclaimed, as she came running over to where Liza, Felicia, Rachel, and I were all standing.

Liza looked curiously at Chloe's red T-shirt — which she was wearing backward, since Thursday was Backward Day of Spirit Week. "You've got some gray hairs on your shirt," she told her.

"I know," Chloe said, nonchalantly brushing the hairs away. "Bud must be shedding."

I almost laughed out loud. Obviously, Chloe had left Bud's hairs on her clothes so someone would ask about them. Actually, knowing Chloe, she might have *put* them on her shirt.

"Who's Bud?" Felicia asked her. She fiddled with her belt buckle, which was digging into her back. "Backward Day is uncomfortable!" she moaned. Then she looked at my hairdo. "You look cute, though."

I tugged slightly at my ponytail — which I'd managed to make come out of the front of my head. Well, sort of. It was actually kind of on the side leaning toward the front, but it was close to being a completely backward ponytail.

"*Bud's* my new dog," Chloe told Felicia proudly.

"You got a dog?" Rachel asked excitedly. "You're so lucky! I've always wanted a dog. Where'd you get Bud?"

"He found me," Chloe told her.

"Huh?" Rachel, Felicia, and Liza wondered.

"He followed me home from Jenny's house yesterday," Chloe explained.

"And your parents are letting you keep him?" Felicia sounded incredulous.

Chloe nodded. "He's mine."

"Until his real owners come to claim him," I reminded Chloe gently. She scowled at me.

"Who're his real owners?" Felicia asked.

Chloe shrugged. "I don't know. He wasn't wearing any tags. He was a stray. Until *now*, that is."

"Oh, the poor thing," Liza said. "He must be so scared."

Chloe shook her head. "No. He's fine. I'm taking really good care of him. I fed him and bathed him last night. And this morning I gave him a long walk before I left for school. He knows he's safe."

"But he doesn't know you or your parents," Liza insisted. "He must be wondering where his real family is."

Chloe bristled at the words. "*We're* his real family now," she told Liza gruffly.

Chloe may have dismissed what Liza had said, but I couldn't. I knew what it felt like to be in a safe place but still miss your house and your family. It's called home-sickness, and I had had a bad case of it the first two nights of overnight camp last summer. I knew I was in a great place, but I still missed my parents, my mice, and my bed. It was a really awful feeling. Poor Bud.

"Have you done anything to let his owners know Bud's safe?" I asked Chloe.

Chloe sighed. "No. Besides, who says he has real owners? Plenty of dogs are just strays. Maybe Bud is one of them."

"He probably is," I agreed. "But we should at least try."

"Really, Chloe, you have to," Felicia insisted. "I know I'd be devastated if Bruno ran away and the people who found him didn't at least *try* to contact me."

I nodded in agreement, knowing how much Felicia loved her dog Bruno.

"We can make posters and put them on telephone poles all over town," Liza suggested.

"And in the park, too," Felicia agreed.

From the look on Chloe's face, I could tell she didn't want to do that at all. Not that I blamed her. She'd already fallen in love with Bud. I knew how that felt. I loved my mice the same way. Still, I kind of sympathized with Bud, too. He had a right to find his real family. It was only fair.

"Look, Chloe, you have to try," I told her gently. "Chances are Bud really is a stray, and no one will come looking for him. But if you don't put up the signs, you'll always wonder. And you'll always be afraid that one day someone will come to take him away from you. This way, if no one comes to claim Bud in a few days, you'll know for sure that he's yours forever."

Chloe sighed. "I guess you're right," she said quietly.

"Good," I said, giving her an encouraging smile. I turned to Liza, Felicia, and Rachel. "Why don't you guys come with me to Chloe's house after school? We can meet Bud and then put up a few signs."

"Is that okay with you?" Liza asked Chloe.

I blushed slightly. I had invited all those people to Chloe's house without even asking her.

"Sure," Chloe said, sounding far less happy than she had before our conversation. "I'm sure Bud would like to meet all of you."

"We want to meet him, too," I assured Chloe.

That seemed to cheer her up a little bit. But I still felt a little bad. I had just broken one of the unspoken middle school rules.

MIDDLE SCHOOL RULE #28:

WHEN YOUR FRIEND HAS A PROBLEM, BE AS SUPPORTIVE AS YOU CAN — ESPECIALLY IN PUBLIC. A CROWD IS NO PLACE TO DISAGREE. IT WILL ONLY MAKE YOUR FRIEND FEEL WORSE.

Even though we were all friends, I guess I should have left the whole find-Bud's-real-home thing for a private conversation. So I hurried to change the subject to take the attention away from Chloe for a while. "Do you guys all have your hats and pom-poms for the pep rally tomorrow afternoon?" I asked.

Liza nodded excitedly. "And I made matching red-and-white tie-dyed T-shirts for all of us last night." She giggled slightly. "I was out in the backyard for a long time. You should have seen my mom's face when she saw that I had sort of dyed a little bit of the grass red, too."

I could only imagine. Liza's mother takes her garden and backyard *very* seriously.

"Anyway, I convinced her it was all for school spirit, and that made her less mad," Liza said. "My mom was a cheerleader in high school, so she sort of gets it."

But only *sort of*, I imagined. No mother — not even one who had been a high school cheerleader — could imagine what it was like to be a student at Joyce Kilmer Middle School this week. There was more to this than school spirit. Deep down, we all knew we were trying to out-spirit the Pops. Once again, it was the Pops against the rest of us. But that was the Pops' fault. They'd started it all, with their matching uniforms. I really hated the way they always thought they had to top everyone else. Of course, they wouldn't be the Pops if they didn't do everything a little bit better than the rest of us, would they? And we wouldn't be us if we didn't try to beat them, anyway. I glanced over at their backward T-shirts and baseball caps. So far we were tied for originality on Backward Day.

"Sam called me last night and said she found some

red-framed sunglasses at the 99¢ Only Store at the mall. She bought a bunch of them for us to wear at the pep rally," Rachel said.

"Cool!" I exclaimed.

"I love sunglasses," Chloe added. "They make me feel like a movie star."

"What *doesn't* make you feel like a movie star?" Felicia teased. Chloe just laughed.

"Hey, do you know why the teacher wore sunglasses to school?" Rachel asked, a playful smile forming on her lips.

"Why?" Liza asked.

"Because her class was so bright!" Rachel exclaimed. She laughed at her own joke.

The rest of us smiled, just to be polite. But that joke had been unusually bad, even for Rachel.

Suddenly, the first bell rang. "Time to get to class," I said.

"Okay," Felicia said, as she turned toward the building. "I'll see you guys on Chloe's bus this afternoon."

I glanced over at Chloe. She clearly wasn't looking forward to the company.

By the time I got out of school that afternoon, Chloe, Felicia, Rachel, and Liza were already on the bus. Liza was sketching a dog-owner-finding poster.

"It's pretty simple," she said, showing me a piece of notebook paper with some pencil scratches on it. "At the top it will say, 'Is This Your Dog?', and then we'll put a picture of Bud beneath that. Then we'll write Chloe's home phone number."

"Perfect," Rachel told her. "It says it all."

"I like it," Felicia agreed.

Chloe didn't say anything. She just stared out the window. I sat down beside her and tried to make conversation. "After we play with Bud for a while, you're coming over to time Cody and Sam in some more races, right?" I asked her.

Chloe nodded. "Sure." She paused for a second. "You're so lucky, Jenny."

"Why?"

"You got your pets at a pet shop. You don't have to go through all of this," she explained. "And besides, they're mice. No one would come looking for them. There are a million mice out there."

Whoa! Now *that* was insulting. There might have been plenty of mice out there, but none of them were *my* mice. I would be devastated if someone tried to take them away from me. Which is exactly why I didn't say anything mean back to Chloe. I knew how she felt. She'd had Bud for less than a day, but I could tell she was already attached to him. And I didn't want to make her any more upset than she clearly was already. As the bus pulled out of the parking lot, I crossed my fingers for Chloe. I really hoped Bud would be hers to keep.

Chapter
SIX

'THAT'S WEIRD,' I murmured as I arrived at the bus stop on Friday morning.

Addie was already there, chatting away on her cell phone. "Well, it's finally happened, Dana," she said loudly. "Jenny McAfee has cracked up. She's talking to herself."

I blushed really red. I had no idea that I'd been talking out loud. But I really *had* been surprised when I got to the bus stop. The missing dog sign I'd put up on the telephone pole near the bus stop was gone. Someone had torn it down during the night. The one I'd taped to the mailbox across the street was gone, too.

"Who would have done that?" I wondered, apparently out loud again, since Addie snickered and turned her back to me so she could whisper into her phone privately. She was probably making plans for this afternoon's pep rally. From the look of the giant bag she was carrying, I could tell the Pops had something big planned.

But I didn't care at all about what Addie was saying. I had more important things to worry about. I couldn't imagine why anyone would take down our signs about Bud. Who wouldn't want a dog to find his home again?

I wasn't the only one wondering, either. When I got to

school, I discovered that every sign between my house and Chloe's had been torn down during the night. Liza, Rachel, and Felicia had noticed the exact same thing as they'd come to school.

"All the signs are gone," Rachel confirmed. "My bus goes through the park, and I didn't see them anywhere."

"There were none on my block, either," Felicia told me. She sighed heavily. "All that work for nothing."

"Maybe not," Liza added hopefully. "It's possible Bud's real owners saw the signs and took them down because they're going to come and get him."

I sighed heavily as I spotted Chloe walking toward us. I wasn't sure if having Bud's real owners call for him would be good news or bad. I guessed it would be both. Good for Bud, but awful for Chloe.

As Chloe walked over to where we were standing, she yawned and blinked her eyes a few times. "Hi, guys," she murmured sleepily.

"Hey, Chloe." I wasn't sure what to say next. Bringing up the posters would just make her sad.

Felicia, however, didn't seem to feel the same way. She had no problem asking Chloe about the missing posters. "Say, were the posters we put up near your house still there this morning? Because the ones near my bus stop . . ."

"I didn't notice." Chloe shrugged and changed the subject. "I was too busy getting ready for this pep rally today to even think about those stupid posters." She perked up noticeably at just the thought of this afternoon's Spirit Week finale. "You guys, we are *so* going to be the most spirited kids in the whole room. We've got everything covered — T-shirts, sunglasses, pom-poms, and hats. I'm telling you — the Pops are going *down*."

"It's not a competition," I reminded her. Then I laughed a little bit. I'd said the words, but I didn't really believe them. And neither did Chloe. We both knew better.

Chloe snickered. "Yeah, right," she said with a laugh.

It was a good thing Spirit Week really *wasn't* a competition. Because if it had been, it would have definitely been a close call between the Pops and my friends. Once again, Addie and her friends were in their "uniforms." But they'd also painted their faces and nails, and this time they were all holding cherry-red megaphones — just so they could be the loudest people cheering at the pep rally.

And people really *were* cheering. They were also clapping and stomping their feet. The noise was so loud in the gym that even though Principal Gold was using a microphone, she had to shout to be heard over us. "Please rise for our school song," she shouted over the PA system. It took a few minutes, but eventually we all quieted down long enough to stand and sing our school song.

> *Sing out for Joyce Kilmer Middle School.*
> *In the crown our school is the jewel.*
> *We will strive to make our voices soar*

So our name will live forever more.
Sing out Kilmer. Be proud of our school. . . .

As I sang the school song, I looked around the gym. Most of the kids were just sort of standing there. They didn't know the words to the song at all. Even my friends were just mumbling syllables that sounded like the words of the song but weren't exactly right. Was it possible that I was the only one who knew our school song word-for-word? Was I the only one who had ever actually read the middle school handbook they give out at orientation? It sure seemed that way at the moment.

"GOOOOO LIONS!" The Pops cheered into their megaphones as the song ended.

"Lions ROAR!" My friends and I cheered back, waving our pom-poms wildly.

"Lions! Lions! Lions!" A group of eighth graders at the top of the bleachers screamed, adding to the spirit.

"I hope Marc's getting this all on film," Josh said, shouting so he could be heard over all the cheering.

"Where is he?" I asked, scanning the crowd for my filmmaker friend.

"Down there, near the basketball hoops," Josh said, pointing down toward the gym floor.

Sure enough, there he was, with his camera in hand, catching all of the craziness for his film — and probably for the school website as well. The kids in the film club usually filmed all of our school events for the site.

"Let me hear you ROAR!" Principal Gold called into her microphone.

"ROAR!" the kids all called back to her.

"Louder!" the principal urged.

"ROAR!" we shouted.

I smiled really broadly. This was my first pep rally. And it was amazing. I'd never heard so much happy noise before. Not even at camp during color war, because then we were all outside. Here, we were in the gym. There was nowhere for the sound to go. All the cheers kept bouncing off the walls and back into the gym. It was really incredible.

"ROAR!" I screamed at the top of my lungs.

At the very second I released my latest lion's roar, our school lion mascot danced out onto the gym floor. Almost immediately, everyone's eyes drifted toward the Pops. We were all looking for the same person — Maya.

I knew Marc wasn't in that costume. He was right there on the gym floor, filming away. And since Maya had been at lunch today, we knew she wasn't absent. So if she was missing now . . .

And she was! The Pops were all sitting together, except for Maya. She was nowhere to be found. Well, that's not really true. Because obviously she *was* in the gym with us. She was dressed as a lion.

The Pops were literally *pop*ping with pride as Maya danced around on the gym floor. They started jumping up and down on the bleachers and screaming into their cherry-red megaphones. "MAYA! MAYA! MAYA!"

Soon other people picked up the same chant. "MAYA! MAYA! MAYA!"

That was really starting to irritate me. We weren't supposed to be cheering for one person, or even one group of friends. We were supposed to be showing *school* spirit.

"We've got spirit . . ." I said loudly to Sam. "Pass it down."

"Got it," Sam agreed. She turned and passed the message to Carolyn. I watched as Carolyn whispered the message to her sister, who sent it over to Liza, who then told Chloe. Meanwhile, I told Josh, who told Felicia, who told Rachel. And on the count of three, we started to cheer really loudly, "We've got spirit! Come on, let's hear it!"

"Go Lions!" a group of kids in front of us chanted loudly.

"A little louder," we called back to them.

"Go Lions!" the group cheered. And this time more kids joined in.

"GO LIONS!" I chanted back, adding my shouts to the roar of our school. "GO LIONS!"

"Blimey! I've never seen anything like that!" Sam exclaimed, as my group of friends walked out of the gym together at the end of the day.

"Me neither," I told her.

"That was the best pep rally ever," Marilyn said.

"Totally," Carolyn agreed.

"Last year's was fun, but nothing like this," Liza told us sixth graders. "I hate to say it, but Maya coming out in that lion costume really put it over the top."

I nodded. The pep rally had been incredible. And there was still a definite buzz in the air. As usual, most of it was focused on the Pops. One by one, people were walking up to Maya and congratulating her on her appearance at the pep rally. But surprisingly, Maya wasn't taking any credit for her performance. In fact, she was denying that she had ever been inside the costume.

"Me? In that ratty old thing?" I heard her ask a crowd of non-Pop seventh graders. "You must be kidding."

"But everyone said it was you. And you weren't at the Pep Rally," a sixth grader named Kia told her.

"I was there," Maya insisted. "I just got to the gym late, so I couldn't sit with my friends."

"Come on, Maya," Dana urged her. "Admit it. You were in the costume. You were terrific."

"Of course she was," Sabrina agreed. "Are we ever anything less?"

I rolled my eyes. I could think of a few times the Pops had been less than terrific. But if I mentioned any of them, I would have had to admit that I was eavesdropping on their conversation. And I didn't want to give the Pops the satisfaction of knowing that.

"I'm not the lion," Maya told the crowd surrounding her. "How could I be? The lion is right there. And I'm standing here."

I turned around to see where Maya was pointing. Sure enough there was the lion mascot again. And she was right. It couldn't be her in there. Not even Houdini could have pulled off a magic trick like that.

It wasn't any of the other Pops, either. They were all standing around Maya, and like the rest of us, they had a surprised look on their faces. This was one big mystery. A mystery the Pops had no interest in solving. After all, if it didn't involve one of them, they couldn't care less.

Neither could anyone else. Without the Pops' seal of approval, the lion had — once again — lost its cool. In fact, instead of cheering for the mascot, the other kids around us were basically ignoring it and boarding the buses to go home.

My cell phone rang at about eight o'clock Friday night. I looked at the name in the caller ID box. Chloe.

"Hey, Chlo," I greeted her. "What's up?"

Chloe answered me, but I had no idea what she was saying. She was crying so hard, her words weren't making any sense at all.

"Whoa, Chloe, calm down," I urged. "I can't understand you."

Nothing but sobs came from the other end of the phone.

"Take a deep breath," I told her. "A *really* deep one."

I could hear Chloe gasping for air — like someone who'd been drowning. Which I guess was what Chloe was doing — drowning in her own tears, that is. Finally, she spoke. "Well, it's happened," she told me. "You guys got your wish."

"What wish?" I asked her. "What guys?"

"You, Liza, Felicia, and Rachel," Chloe told me. "You got what you wanted. Bud just left . . . with his *real* family."

"Oh," I said quietly. I felt just awful for my friend. I knew that Bud's real owners were really happy right now. And Bud probably was, too. We'd done the right thing. But listening to Chloe sob on the other end of the phone confused me. Suddenly, doing the right thing didn't seem so right.

"I don't know how they found him," Chloe cried. "I mean, I thought I had taken all the signs down when I took Bud for his walk last night."

"*You?*" I asked. Then I shut my mouth tight. The last thing Chloe needed was me yelling at her about taking down all of our signs. Obviously it hadn't mattered, anyway. Bud was back where he belonged. "Was Bud happy to see his family?" I asked her tentatively.

"His name isn't Bud," Chloe corrected me. "It's Fred. And the minute they walked in the door, he bolted right to them and never looked back. He was kind of ungrateful, if you ask me."

"Do they know how he disappeared?" I asked her.

"They said that he was out in their yard, and one of their friends left the gate open. Bud — I mean *Fred* — likes to chase squirrels. He must've chased one over a few of the neighbors' yards, and then gotten lost. Apparently, he's been missing for a week."

"They must have been happy you took such good care of him," I told Chloe gently.

"Yeah. My folks were pretty impressed, too," Chloe admitted. "My mom said that now that she's seen how responsible I am with a pet, I can get one of my own. She said we could even go to the shelter tomorrow and pick one out."

"Oh, Chloe! That's wonderful!" I exclaimed.

"I guess." Chloe sounded less sure. "But no matter what pet I bring home, it won't be Bud."

"I know," I said kindly. "But this pet will really be yours. And you can choose the kind of animal that you want. One that fits you."

"I don't know what kind of pet would fit me," Chloe said, her voice slowly gaining a little bit of excitement.

"We can figure it out together," I promised her. "There must be some quiz on middleschoolsurvival.com that could help us. I'll come over first thing in the morning and we'll take the quiz together."

"Do we have to wait until tomorrow morning?" Chloe asked.

"Huh?"

"Well, that's the other reason I'm calling," she explained. "I'm lonely without Bud here. My mom and dad said you could sleep over — if it's okay with your parents."

"I'll ask them right now," I said excitedly. "I'm sure they'll say yes!"

An hour later, I was sitting next to Chloe in her family room, staring at the computer screen. Once again, my favorite website had come to the rescue. We'd found the perfect quiz to help Chloe with her dilemma.

Meow! Tweet! Woof! Which Pet Is Best for You?

Before you run off to the pet shop (or the shelter) to pick out the perfect pet, you should be sure you're getting an animal that will fit in with your family. Having a pet can be a lot of fun, but it's also a big responsibility. So before you look into those cages and fall in love with a pair of big brown (or green, or blue) eyes, take this simple quiz.

1. How much time do you have to spend with your pet?

A. A lot of time

B. Some time

C. Not much time at all

Chloe sat there and stared at the screen for a very long time. I could tell she was taking this very seriously. Having a pet was a big responsibility. She wanted to do what was right.

"Well, I can be with my pet before and after school, and on the weekends," Chloe said out loud. "I don't mind hanging out at home. You guys could come over and play with my new pet a lot, too." She was quiet for a minute, thinking about the rest of her schedule. "But there's no one home during the day. And next year, I want to be in the school play again, so I might have to stay after school sometimes. . . ." Her voice drifted off for a second as she studied the options on the screen. Finally, she clicked the letter B.

A moment later, the next question popped up on the computer screen.

2. How clean do you like your house?

A. My family doesn't mind a mess.
B. We're fine with some mess, but we clean it up regularly.
C. We like it clean around here.

"I'd say B again," Chloe said. "It gets kind of cluttered around here. But we're not dirty or anything. And Bud didn't make things any worse."

I noticed that Chloe was still calling Fred, "Bud." I guessed she probably always would. There was no reason to point it out to her, though. It wasn't hurting anyone.

"Letter B it is," I said. Chloe clicked her mouse over the right square, and waited for the next question.

3. How tolerant are you of noise?

    A. We're a loud family; a little more noise won't make any difference.

    B. Some animal noise would be fine, as long as it's not constant.

    C. My folks like it to be quiet when they're home.

I started to giggle. The answer to this question was obvious. At the moment, Chloe's dad was in the basement, banging on a drum kit. We were in the family room, doing a quiz and listening to some tunes Chloe had downloaded. And her mom was upstairs dancing around to an exercise DVD. I wasn't at all surprised when Chloe clicked on the letter A. Noise didn't bother this family one bit.

4. How interactive would you like to be with your pet?

    A. Very. I want a pet that will be my best friend.

    B. Somewhat. I want to be able to hang out with my pet — just not all the time.

    C. Not very. I like watching animals more than playing with them.

"Well, I have plenty of really good friends," Chloe said, smiling at me. "But you can't have too many. It would be nice to have a pet that I could call my best friend."

"When I got Cody and Sam I already had a best friend," I said quietly. "In fact, Addie was with me when I went to the pet store and picked them out."

Chloe gave me an understanding smile. "I guess animals are more loyal than people," she told me.

I smiled back. "Not always," I assured her. "Just in Addie's case."

"I still don't get how you two were ever friends, never mind *best* friends," Chloe said.

I thought about trying to explain how different the old Addie was from the Pop princess Chloe knew. But it wasn't worth it. She'd probably never believe me, anyway. Addie had changed far too much. "Forget Addie. Just pick an answer," I said finally.

Chloe clicked on A. "I want a best friend," she said definitively.

5. Do you want a pet you can train?

A. Absolutely!

B. It would be fun to teach a pet a few tricks, but I don't have the patience for much more.

C. It's not necessary.

"I already know it's fun to train a pet," Chloe told me. "I mean look at all the fun we're having training Cody and Sam to go through mazes."

I grinned as Chloe clicked on the box beside the letter A. It was hard to believe that less than a week ago Chloe hated the very sight of my mice. Now she was admitting it was fun working with them. Apparently, the mice weren't the only ones who'd been taught some new behaviors.

A message popped up on the screen. The quiz was over. It was time to find out what kind of pet would be best for Chloe.

You gave three A answers and two B answers. So what kind of furry, finned, or feathered friend is best for you? Check the chart and find out.

If you answered mostly As:
Laid-back types who have time to hang out with their pets and won't mind a bit of a mess and noise might consider adopting a dog or a parrot. Both of these pets like having people around as much as possible. Both parrots and dogs can be taught all kinds of tricks, and they like to be handled by the people they love most. However, parrots and dogs both tend to be messy (dogs shed, and parrots spit seeds all over the place), so you have to be tolerant of that.

If you answered mostly Bs:
A cat or a rabbit would be a good pet for you. Both of these animals like human companionship, but they're not in almost constant need of it, the way dogs and parrots are. Both bunnies and cats can be taught simple tricks, but it takes a lot of work. While there is some mess involved in keeping these furry folks in your house, it's not as extreme as some other

pets. Cats will clean themselves, unlike dogs who require baths. But remember that litter boxes and rabbit cages have to be cleaned regularly.

If you answered mostly Cs: If you don't have a lot of time to spend with your pet, but you'd really like to add a little animal fun to your life, consider a canary, gerbil, tortoise, or tropical fish. As a rule, canaries are content to stay in their cages and sing (just make sure the cage is large enough to be comfortable for your bird). They don't particularly care for human contact. The same goes for tortoises, who like to walk around the yard from time to time, but don't need to be pet or handled on a regular basis. Gerbils (or mice or hamsters) are happy to stay in their cages, running on their wheels, or playing in plastic climbing-gyms you can construct. However, gerbils, mice, and hamsters are nocturnal, which means they like to play when you like to sleep. Tropical fish are beautiful, and very calming to watch.

"A dog or a parrot," Chloe mused, reading the section that was for people who answered with mostly As. "I never thought about getting a bird."

"Birds are pretty," I said. "And you can teach them to talk."

"But you can't cuddle up with a parrot," Chloe pointed out. "And they don't sleep with you at night."

"You really want a dog, don't you?" I asked her.

Chloe nodded. "I think I knew that all along. I just took the quiz to make sure I was doing the right thing."

"You are," I assured her. "Any dog would be lucky to have you for a friend."

Chloe nodded. "Thanks," she told me. "I'm lucky to have *you* for a friend."

"Right back at you," I assured her.

"So tomorrow we'll go to the pound and see if there are any dogs there who are looking for a family," Chloe said.

"I'm sure there are," I told her. "But once you're there, the hard part starts."

"What's that?" she asked me.

"Finding the right dog," I told her. "You can't take them all home."

Chloe nodded. "And knowing me, I'm going to want to."

Chapter
SEVEN

CHLOE WASN'T KIDDING. From the minute we entered the animal shelter, she was *oohing* and *aahing* over every dog we came in contact with. "They're all so cute," she cooed. "How am I ever going to choose just one?"

"You'll know which dog is the right one," I assured Chloe.

"How?" she wondered.

I shrugged. "You'll just know," I said.

"Oooh, look at those puppies," Chloe cooed, pointing to a cage where three little cocker spaniel puppies were all curled up together.

"No puppies," Chloe's mom reminded her. "We talked about this. I don't want to start with toilet training again. It was hard enough training you."

Chloe blushed beet-red. I thought it was funny that I'd never seen her blush before. Chloe wasn't usually embarrassed. Until now. Not that I blamed her. Having your mom talk about toilet training in front of your friends is incredibly embarrassing.

"Let's try those cages over there." I pointed to a group of crates at the other end of the shelter. I wanted to change the subject as quickly as possible.

"Yeah." Chloe smiled gratefully. "Great idea."

We walked down the aisle, looking into each cage. There were puppies in most of the cages, and we already knew they were out of the question. Then we came upon a cage toward the end of the row. Inside was a medium-size white, black, and brown dog. Chloe and I stopped at his cage and read the card on the door.

Terrier mix. 2 years old. Male.

"Oh, he's adorable," Chloe cooed. She kneeled down to get a closer look at the frightened pooch. I watched as the terrier picked up his head and glanced curiously in Chloe's direction.

"Don't be scared, little guy," Chloe said in a soft, gentle tone I'd never heard her use before. "I won't hurt you."

Something in her voice must have attracted the dog, because he slowly rose to his feet and tentatively padded over to where Chloe was kneeling. He put his face up to the bars and sniffed at her. Then he reached out his tongue and licked her on the cheek.

"I found him!" Chloe squealed. The dog was slightly surprised by her sudden excitement, but he didn't bark. He just cocked his head slightly and opened his eyes wider.

A moment later, Chloe's mother and one of the attendants at the animal shelter were standing beside us.

"Are you sure?" Chloe's mom asked her.

Chloe nodded. "This is my dog. I can just tell. We were meant to be together." Chloe turned to me. "You were right. I knew it right away. And so did he."

"Is this dog good with children?" Chloe's mother asked the attendant.

"Terriers are good pets for families," the woman replied. "And this fellow has been especially mellow the whole time he's been here."

"And he's trained?" Chloe's mother asked. "To go outside, I mean."

The attendant nodded. "Completely. He was owned by a couple who had to move. Their new building didn't allow pets. He's been very well trained and cared for."

"And he still will be," Chloe promised. "I won't let anything happen to him." She turned to me. "Thanks so much for coming with me, Jenny. Bingo and I will always remember you were here on the day we found each other."

"Bingo?" I asked her.

Chloe nodded. "That's what I'm naming him. Like the dog in the song."

I laughed. It wasn't the most original name in the world, but it definitely fit him. In fact, everything today just seemed to fit together.

"I'm really happy for you," I told Chloe.

"I'm happy for me, too," Chloe said. "In fact, I think this is the happiest I've ever been."

The whole next week, Chloe split her after-school time between her house and mine. Every day, she hurried home to walk and play with Bingo. And then, as soon as her mom got home from work, she would drive Chloe to my house so we could work on our science project. Then we spent the next hour or so tracking the time it took for Cody and Sam to run in their mazes and writing the times down on the poster board we'd gotten from the art teacher.

All that hard work really paid off. On the morning of the science fair we were ready to show off our experiment to everyone in the school. We had our poster tacked up to the wall and the mazes laid out on tables. Cody and Sam were in their cage, ready to be placed in their mazes to run as soon as it was our turn to present our project. My dad had even driven me to school on the way to work in the morning so I wouldn't have to take them on the bus.

I glanced around the cafeteria, which was where the science fair was being held. A few tables down I spotted Liza and Chuck's project. They'd done an experiment on how IMing affects people's ability to concentrate. Turns out that if you're zapping messages to your friends, your homework suffers. It wasn't exactly an earth-shattering discovery, but Liza had used her art talent to decorate their poster with drawings of kids at their computer keyboards, so their project looked really cool.

Addie and Dana's table was next to Liza and Chuck's. Their presentation was called: WHAT MAKES WATERPROOF MAKEUP WATERPROOF? I rolled my eyes when I caught sight of their poster. Leave it to two Pops to figure out a way to turn makeup into science.

I'm sure Addie and Dana thought that was a topic everyone would be interested in, but it actually *wasn't* the table everyone seemed to be buzzing about. Instead, it was Josh and Felicia's. Their project was still a big mystery. Whatever they'd created was *huge*. It took up most of the table, and stood at least three feet tall. But it was impossible to tell exactly what it was, because the project was covered by a thick, black cloth. Everyone was dying to know what was under there. We all knew for sure that it was probably amazing, since Josh-the-genius had built it (along with Felicia, of course).

My attention drifted from Josh and Felicia, though, the minute Marc walked into the cafeteria. He was carrying a laptop computer and his camera. But that wasn't what caught my eye. It was the fact that Marc was with Maya. Their appearance together caught Chloe by surprise as well.

"Poor Marc," Chloe said with a sigh. "Maya's been his partner. That must've really stunk."

She wasn't kidding. Working with a Pop on a project had to have been a nightmare. I couldn't imagine what topic Marc and Maya could ever have agreed on. After all, it wasn't like Marc was going to want to work on something Pop-like. And I couldn't imagine Maya working on anything that didn't involve makeup or fashion.

"I want to go over and see what they did," I told Chloe. "Can you stay here with the mice?"

"Sure," Chloe agreed. "I'll fill the water bottles in the mazes."

"Thanks," I said. "I'll come right back and then you can

have a turn to walk around and see what everyone has worked on."

As I dashed across the gym, I noticed other people were heading in Marc and Maya's direction. No surprise there. The idea of a Pop and a non-Pop working together on a project was kind of a novelty in our school. Of course, it was only happening because seventh graders were assigned partners instead of being allowed to choose them. Still, I figured it would be interesting to see what they could come up with together, and apparently so did everyone else.

Maya was hanging up their poster when I reached their table. It said, THE EFFECTS OF PEER INFLUENCE ON GROUP REACTIONS.

I couldn't imagine what that meant. I knew what peer pressure was and all that, but I just couldn't figure out exactly what Maya and Marc had been testing. At least not until Marc began playing the DVD he'd made. Once the image of the lion mascot appeared on the screen of his laptop, it all became clear.

The footage was of the first time we'd seen the lion — in the cafeteria during fifth period lunch. I vaguely remembered Marc filming that day, but I'd figured he was just making his movie. I had no idea the footage was for his science project.

"A positive reaction from people who others look up to caused students to view the lion mascot in a positive light." Marc's voice was coming from the DVD. "However, when the same group later discovered that it was not one of their friends in the suit, their reaction changed. The reaction of the other students then changed as well." The image on the screen switched. Instead of showing the lion in the cafeteria, it showed the bored reaction of students in the parking lot as the same mascot appeared there. One student could even be heard murmuring, "That thing is so lame."

I made my way through the crowd of kids and went over to where Marc was standing. "So it *was* you in the costume," I said to him.

"Some of the time," he admitted. "And some of the time it was Maya. We wanted to prove that people change their minds about what's cool and what's not due to the influence of certain people."

"How'd you come up with that?" I asked him.

"I didn't," he replied.

"*Maya* came up with the idea?" I was shocked.

Marc shook his head. "No. Mrs. Arlington did. She thought it would be an interesting topic. And since Maya and I couldn't agree on anything else, we just went with it."

"Mrs. Arlington knows about the Pops?" I asked him, surprised. I didn't think teachers had any clue about the social structure in the school. I figured they just stuck to teaching and ignored everything else.

Marc nodded. "I think she does know," he said, sounding every bit as incredulous as I felt. "But she never said that exactly. She just said she wondered if people would react differently to the mascot if they thought their friend was inside."

And boy did they, I thought. But that wasn't the most interesting part of the experiment. At least not to me. "I still can't believe you let Maya use your video camera," I noted.

"Are you nuts?" Marc asked me. "I wouldn't let her near my camera."

"But if you were inside the lion suit, who shot the video of the kids' reactions?" I wondered.

"I did," Marc said. "There's a hole where the lion's mouth is. That's what you look out of when you're inside. So when it was my turn to wear the suit, I just held the camera up and shot the footage through the hole."

"Pretty clever," I told him.

"I thought so," he agreed. "It kept my camera safe, anyway."

"I guess you proved that if the Pops think something is cool, then everyone else will say it's cool, too, just to be like the Pops," I said.

Marc nodded. "Not like we needed to do a science project to figure that out," he said. "We live it every day. But I guess Mrs. Arlington thought it would be interesting. And besides, Maya and I came to an interesting conclusion."

"What?" I asked him.

"That peer pressure isn't always bad. When people thought the lion was cool, they were more interested in Spirit Week," Marc told me. "It's kind of like celebrities coming out for causes like solving global warming or helping poor people in Africa. Other people will do the same thing to be like the celebrities."

I nodded. Marc wasn't far off. In our school, the Pops were the stars. And since Marc had been working with one of them, I wondered if he liked being in their orbit. "So are you and Maya friends now?" I wondered.

Marc shook his head. "Are you kidding? She's a pain in the neck. She kept complaining that being inside the costume was too hot and her makeup was running. I couldn't believe what a big deal she made out of that."

I opened my mouth to say something else, but my words were drowned out by screams coming from the other side of the cafeteria.

"MOUSE!" I heard someone yell.

"Catch him!" someone else shouted.

I turned around just in time to see Dana leap up on a chair and Chloe burst into tears.

"Oh, no! My mice!" I cried. I zoomed across the cafeteria as fast as I could.

"Jenny, I'm so sorry," Chloe blubbered. "Sandee Wind came by and said the mice were disgusting and I wanted to show her they weren't, so I took Cody out of his cage and . . ."

I didn't hear the rest of what she was saying. I couldn't concentrate on anything but the fact that Cody had obviously run away. And I had to find him. The thought of my poor little mouse loose in that big cafeteria, with people screaming and yelling, was horrifying. He was probably petrified.

I was mad at Chloe. Furious even. But this was no time for me to deal with her. Right now I had to find Cody!

"Oh, no. There he goes!" I heard someone yell from near the windows. I dashed in the direction of the scream.

"Yikes!" an eighth grader shouted a moment later, as she leaped up onto a table. "I hate mice."

Just then, Addie ran past me at top speed. I saw her crouch down on the floor. A moment later she stood up. Her hands were cupped, and she was walking toward me.

"I've got him," she called over to me. "Relax, Jenny."

I could feel the tears welling up in my eyes. Now that Cody was safe, I could allow myself to cry. How weird was that? Probably not as weird as the fact that it had been Addie Wilson who'd saved him!

Apparently, I wasn't the only one who thought that was out of the ordinary. A few minutes later, as I was placing Cody safely back into his cage, Sabrina Rosen came running over to where Addie and I were standing.

"I can't believe you held that creepy thing in your hands," Sabrina told Addie. She glanced in my direction and sneered. "And why would you help *her*?"

Addie didn't answer. She didn't have to. I already knew why. Addie and I might not be friends anymore, but we had been — for a very long time. She'd spent plenty of hours playing with Cody and Sam in my room. She didn't want to see anything happen to Cody, regardless of whether or not we were still BFF.

"Thanks, Addie," I murmured quietly.

"No big deal." Addie shrugged and turned to Sabrina. "Let's go see what Maya's project is. There's a huge crowd around her table." And with that, she was gone.

It took a few minutes before Chloe could even look at me. Finally, she whispered, "I'm sorry, Jenny. I really am."

I could have yelled at Chloe. I could have told her that she'd been really irresponsible with my pets. I could have asked her how she would have felt if I'd left her door open and Bingo had escaped and run away. But there wasn't any point in saying any of that. She looked upset enough as it was. And it wasn't like she'd let Cody run away on purpose. In fact, she'd been defending him when it happened.

"It's okay," I told my friend. "He's safe now."

But just because I wasn't mad anymore, it didn't mean I was taking any chances that it would happen again. "Why don't you go look around the science fair for a while?" I suggested to Chloe. "I'll hang out here and keep an eye on Sam and Cody. They'd probably feel safer with me around, anyway."

Chloe nodded. "That's true," she admitted. "I do want to find out what Josh and Felicia have under that cloth."

"Let me know if they tell you," I said. "I'm really curious."

And I wasn't the only one. There was quite a commotion

going on at their table. And from where I was standing, I could pretty much see and hear the whole thing.

"Come on, just take the cloth off," I heard Dana say to Josh and Felicia.

"Not yet," Josh told her. "We're waiting until it's our turn. But I can promise you this — our project will blow the roof off this place."

I smiled. It was good to hear Josh holding his own against Dana. She could be kind of a bully when she wanted to be. Like now, for instance.

"Oh, give me a break," she groaned. "How big of a surprise could it be? I mean, it's just some geeky science project." And with that she pulled the cloth right off of their project.

I was kind of surprised to see what was under that cloth. And disappointed, too. From where I was standing, it didn't seem that amazing.

Dana didn't think so, either. "A volcano?" she asked. "What's the big deal about that? I did a project on volcanoes in the fourth grade. And I showed what it looked like from the *inside*."

"We show what it looks like on the inside," Felicia told her. She pointed to the poster she and Josh had put together. "See?"

Dana laughed right in Felicia's face. "I thought your boyfriend was supposed to be a real science geek," she said. Then she turned around to make sure everyone around could hear her. "But I guess he's just a geek."

"Dana, watch your hand!" Josh exclaimed. But it was too late. At that moment, the volcano on the table started to rumble and shake. And then, without warning, it erupted – sending reddish brown goo flying into the air! A second later, the lava-like goo was raining down all over Dana.

"Now look what you've done!" Dana shouted at Felicia and Josh. "This was a brand-new dress. I bought it just for the science fair." She tried to run her fingers through her usually smooth hair. But now her hair was all chunky and thick with red gunk. "And how am I supposed to get this junk out of my hair?"

"Try peanut butter," I heard Sam say in her British accent.

Dana glared at her.

"What?" Sam asked her. "It works for gum. Maybe it works for fake lava, too."

I giggled at the thought of Dana walking around school covered in gooey lava and smelling like a peanut butter sandwich. Of course, if Marc's peer influence science project was any indication, peanut butter might become the most popular perfume in the school if she did.

"This is all your fault!" Dana screamed at Felicia and Josh.

"I told you to watch your hand," Josh told Dana. "You leaned right on the activation button. You made our volcano erupt!"

From the look on Dana's face, I could tell *she* was about

to erupt — with anger. But before she could, Mrs. Johnson hurried over to the table.

"We were going to take this outside like you told us to," Felicia swore, "but Dana . . ."

Mrs. Johnson nodded. "I saw what happened," she told Felicia kindly. Then she turned to Dana. "They asked you not to touch their project," she reminded her.

"But . . ." Dana murmured feebly. There wasn't much she could say. As Mrs. Johnson had told Felicia, she'd seen the whole thing. Which meant she knew Dana was completely to blame.

"You've got to clean this up, Dana," Mrs. Johnson told her.

Dana looked around at the mounds of reddish brown gunk all over the cafeteria floor. It was already hardening. Cleaning it up wasn't going to be an easy job, and she knew it.

"Maybe a few of your friends will help you," Mrs. Johnson suggested.

But Dana's friends were nowhere to be found. They'd all scurried back to their projects the minute the explosion had occurred. As Dana looked hopefully around the cafeteria for a volunteer, the Pops turned away, pretending to busy themselves with their posters and projects. Dana was on her own.

As Dana hurried to the janitor's closet for a mop, I almost felt bad for her. It must be hard not to have friends you can actually count on when you need them. I thought about the millions of times my friends and I had helped one another out. We were always there for one another, no matter what.

We might not have the power to turn an old lion mascot into the star of Spirit Week, but we were powerful enough to help one another through sticky times. And that was more than Dana could say at the moment. My friends and I made one another happy. And because of that we were all surviving middle school — *together*.

Peer Pressure Cooker

Peer Pressure. It's a middle school tradition. The question is: How do you handle it? Are you the type of person who always marches to the beat of her own drummer, or do you follow in your friends' footsteps? Take this quiz and find out how much pressure you can take.

1. **Woo-hoo! You've been invited to a party — by an eighth grader! Your two BFFs were also invited. Unfortunately, your folks have totally nixed the party, but, your pals have said they'll cover for you if you want to sneak out. What do you do?**

   A. Go get ready. It's time to P-A-R-T-Y!
   B. Stay home, but stomp around angrily all night long.
   C. Invite your two BFFs to sleep at your house and have a slumber party instead. It's a party without pressure!

2. **You're in math class, and the most popular girl in school asks to copy off your test. What's your reaction?**

   A. Cover your paper so she can't cheat.
   B. Move a little closer and let her look — she could be your ticket into the popular crowd.
   C. Make no effort to cover your paper, but don't make it easy for her to look. If she cheats, she cheats. But you're not going to help her do it.

3. You're eating at the food court in the mall. The kids you're with are making fun of what a girl at the next table is wearing. How do you handle this?

A. Tell your friends to cut it out. How would they feel if someone was making fun of them?

B. Sit quietly and eat your food.

C. Join in on the slammin'.

4. It's time to sign up for school clubs. You want to be in the play, but your friends say they won't hang out with "theater geeks." What's your reaction?

A. You sign up for the same club as your pals and take theater classes on the weekends so no one from school will know.

B. You sign up for the cooking club with your pals. Club time is supposed to be a social time after all.

C. Join the school theater club anyway. If your current friends are that judgmental, you'll be better off with a new crowd!

5. Your mom has a rule — no makeup until you're 14. But all the popular girls are wearing it now! What do you do?

A. Follow the no makeup rule, but develop a style all your own that's fresh-faced and fashion forward.

B. Bug your mom until she'll compromise and let you wear clear, shiny lip gloss to school.

C. Keep makeup in your locker. You can put it on in the morning and wash it off before you go home.

6. The guy you're crushing on has made it clear he won't go out with a girl who gets better grades than he does. What do you do?

A. Get your usual good grades, but lie so he thinks he's smarter.

B. Get your usual high marks, and find yourself a new crush.

C. Flunk your next Spanish test on purpose.

7. You know you're not supposed to go into the abandoned lot near the school because your folks think it's dangerous. But a bunch of your friends are having a pick-up softball game there. What's your game plan?

A. Go play all nine innings. Your mom and dad won't know.

B. Forget the game and head home.

C. Play the first two innings, but then head home before it starts getting dark. That's less dangerous, anyway.

8. It's truth or dare time at your weekly Friday night slumber party. You've been dared to call the cutest boy in the grade and tell him you like him. But that would be very, *very* embarrassing! What do you do?

A. Refuse to make the call.

B. Make the call, but give a fake name, hoping he'll never know it's you.

C. Take a deep breath, get ready, dial the digits, and tell the cutie who you are and why you called. It'll be embarrassing, but at least your friends won't think you're a chicken.

Okay, pencils down. The quiz is over. Now it's time to find out just how influenced you are by peer pressure. Start by adding up your score. Then keep reading to find out if peer pressure is running your life.

	A)	B)	C)
1.	A) 3	B) 2	C) 1
2.	A) 1	B) 3	C) 2
3.	A) 1	B) 2	C) 3
4.	A) 2	B) 3	C) 1
5.	A) 1	B) 2	C) 3
6.	A) 2	B) 1	C) 3
7.	A) 3	B) 1	C) 2
8.	A) 1	B) 2	C) 3

19-24 points: Uh-oh! You are far too influenced by what your friends say. In fact, you rarely seem to make your own decisions. It might be hard, but you really do need to start standing up for your own beliefs once in a while. You'll find you'll like yourself a whole lot more.

12-18 points: You are obviously the queen of compromise. You know that sometimes it's easier to go along with the crowd than fight it. But you also know that at times, it's important to stand your ground and do what you think is right. Peer pressure doesn't rule you, but there are times you allow yourself to be influenced by others.

8-11 points: Peer pressure? You're not having it. You are a firm believer in living life on your own terms. That's great, because after all, you're the one who will have to live with the results of your actions, not your friends. Keep on marching to the beat of your own drummer!

NANCY KRULIK HAS WRITTEN more than 150 books for children and young adults, including three *New York Times* bestsellers. She is the author of the popular Katie Kazoo Switcheroo series and is also well known as a biographer of Hollywood's hottest young stars. Her knowledge of the details of celebrities' lives has made her a desired guest on several entertainment shows on the E! network as well as on *Extra* and *Access Hollywood*. Nancy lives in Manhattan with her husband, composer Daniel Burwasser, their two children, Ian and Amanda, and a crazy cocker spaniel named Pepper.